The Chronicles of Paul III:

Road to Nowhere

The Chronicles of Paul III:

Road to Nowhere

Scott M. Baker

Also by Scott M. Baker

Novels
Operation Majestic
The Deadliest Breed of Assassins
Nurse Alissa vs. the Zombies
Nurse Alissa vs. the Zombies: Escape
Nurse Alissa vs. the Zombies III: Firestorm
Nurse Alissa vs. the Zombies IV: Hunters
Nurse Alissa vs. the Zombies V: Desperate Mission
Nurse Alissa vs. the Zombies VI: Rescue
Nurse Alissa vs. the Zombies VII: On the Road
Nurse Alissa vs. the Zombies VIII: New Beginnings
Nurse Alissa vs. the Zombies IX: Calm Before the Storm
The Chronicles of Paul: A Nurse Alissa Spin-Off
The Chronicles of Paul II: Errand of Mercy
The Ghosts of Eden Hollow
The Ghosts of Salem Village
The Ghosts of the Maria Doria
The Ghosts of Bethlehem Asylum
Frozen World
Shattered World I: Paris
Shattered World II: Russia
Shattered World III: China
Shattered World IV: Japan
Shattered World V: Hell
The Vampire Hunters
Vampyrnomicon
Dominion
Rotter World
Rotter Nation

Rotter Apocalypse
Yeitso

Novellas
Nazi Ghouls From Space
Twilight of the Living Dead
This Is Why We Can't Have Nice Things During the Zombie Apocalypse
Dead Water

Anthologies
Crossroads in the Dark V: Beyond the Borders
Rejected for Content
Roots of a Beating Heart
The Zombie Road Fan Fiction Collection
The Collector
Vlada: Tales of the Damned
Through the Aftermath: A Post-Apocalyptic Anthology

A Schattenseite Book

The Chronicles of Paul III: Road to Nowhere
by Scott M. Baker.
Copyright © 2023. All Rights Reserved.
Print Edition
ISBN-13: 979-8-9884973-2-5

Cover Art © Christian Bentulan

To the Wyrd Realities crew, especially Hadley, Allen, and Rich.

I'm so glad you brought me on board.

It has been a great two years.

I've learned a lot and made a lot of good friends.

Chapter One

"**H**ERE YOU GO." The teenager handed Paul a Styrofoam cup of lukewarm coffee.

"Thanks." Paul took it and swirled the coffee around inside the cup.

"Sorry, we don't have any cream or sugar, sir."

"I like my coffee dark and bitter. Like my soul. And please, don't call me sir."

"That's the way my parents raised me." He turned and handed the second cup to Daphne. "Here's yours, ma'am."

"Thanks." Daphne wrapped her fingers around the cup, enjoying the semi-warmth on her fingers. "Your parents raised a good kid."

An expression of despair washed across the teenager's face. "They'd be proud to hear that. I wish they were still with us."

"I'm sorry," said Daphne, her tone sympathetic. "Do you want to talk about it?"

"Not much to talk about. On the first day of the outbreak, my old man came home with a bite on his hand. Said some asshole bit him on the bus. An hour later, he turned and attacked my mother. I grabbed the car keys, rushed my sister out of the house before my parents could get her, and headed north. We joined up with Torosian's group the next day."

"Is your sister safe?" asked Daphne.

"Thank God. Her name is Addison." He pointed to a young girl playing with Judith. "That's her with your daughter."

"That's not our kid," Paul corrected the teenager. "Judith is Lisa's daughter. We saved Lisa on the second day of the outbreak and headed north to rescue her daughter."

"We nearly got killed saving her, too," added Daphne.

"They're lucky you found them."

"Thanks." Paul paused. "What's your name, kid?"

"Jared."

Paul stood and extended his hand. "I'm Paul. This is Daphne. It's a pleasure to meet you."

Jared gave the hand a firm pump. "Likewise."

"You did good saving your sister. You should be proud of yourself."

"I did what anyone would in such a situation."

Daphne shook her head. "You'd be shocked how often it's everyone for themselves."

Polozov, the Russian who operated the Tigercat, approached. "Sorry to interrupt, but we're about to discuss salvage operation."

They joined the others. Everyone except the children gathered outside the trailer, thirty-six people in total, six from Paul's group and twenty-eight from Torosian's. The children sat on the ground a few hundred feet away, playing with Gojira.

Torosian made eye contact with those around him as he spoke. "I don't have to tell you that our situation is desperate. We have the equipment to cut down enough trees to form a log wall around the compound but, other than that, we're in tough shape. We barely have enough food and water to last a day. And we have no medical supplies, extra clothing, weapons, sleeping bags or beds, nothing. If we hope to survive long enough for the government to regain control, assuming they can, we need to stockpile what we need. Any suggestions?"

"What about Leesburg?" suggested Polozov. "There are plenty of stores there."

"It won't work." Paul shook his head. "We barely escaped with our lives. The city is overrun with deaders."

"I was afraid of that." Torosian paused. "Is anyone from around here?"

"I am. I'm Jared. My sister and I used to live in Purcellville."

"Me, too," added an attractive woman a little over five feet in height with blue eyes and long, dark brown hair sprinkled with silver sparkles. "I'm Heather Chargualaf. My hubs and I lived five miles outside of Front Royal."

"Is he here with you?" asked Torosian.

Heather grew solemn. "No. He was a nurse working the midnight shift at Warren Memorial Hospital when the outbreak occurred. He called to tell me things were really bad, and he'd be home as soon as possible. When I didn't hear from him after two days, I headed into town to rescue him. The hospital was overrun by the living dead. I hit the road and wound up here."

"I'm sorry," said Torosian. "If it's any consolation, none of us have heard from our families since this shit began."

Paul thought about Alissa and wondered if she had made it out of Boston alive.

"What's the situation like in Front Royal?" asked Donnelly, who operated the crusher.

Heather sighed. "Not good. From what little I saw, the entire town was swarming with the living dead. Trying to do a supply run there would be suicide."

"Are there any other towns nearby?" asked Torosian.

"Several," Jared answered. "If you're looking for large stores to raid, there's a Walmart Supercenter and Target in Winchester."

"We came from Pittsburgh," said Daphne. "Every town we passed through was infested, so I'm not sure it's worth the risk."

"There are several grocery stores, Lowes, and Home Depots in the smaller towns," offered Jared.

"I'm sure they were looted on day one," said Paul. "Even if there's anything left worth salvaging, chances are those places are swarming with deaders."

Torosian sighed. "Then we're screwed."

"Not necessarily," said Heather. "A FedEx distribution facility opened last year right outside of Philomont. I used to work there part-time. People do all their shopping online now. Everything we need passes through there, including firearms."

"No." The adamant response came from a slim, middle-aged woman with a blonde bob. She shook her head violently. "I don't want to be around weapons. They're dangerous."

A young brunette shook her head. "In case you haven't figured it out yet, so are the deaders."

The middle-aged woman bristled. "Who do you think you are talking to me that way?"

The brunette got into the woman's face. "Someone who wants to survive and is smart enough to know we don't have a chance if we're unarmed."

"I refuse to be part of the gun culture."

Groans and protests came from the rest of the group. Torosian raised his hand to quiet them down, then focused his attention on the blonde.

"Shut the fuck up, Pam. We need weapons to survive. You're welcome to hit the road if you don't like it. No one will stop you."

The rest of Torosian's people mumbled in agreement.

Pam lowered her head and moved back to the outer fringes of the meeting. Torosian glared at her, then turned his attention back to Heather.

"Won't the facility be overrun by deaders like everything else?"

"I doubt it. A fence surrounds the compound, and the only access is through a guarded security gate. The building itself has steel doors that are locked from the inside. It's a private facility, so few people know about it. Plus, it's out in the middle of nowhere, so I doubt there are many deaders around, if any."

"We'd have to take every car parked on the road to gather

enough supplies," said Ed.

"Not necessarily. They usually bring the packages from the airport in tractor-trailers. There's always at least half a dozen at the facility at any given time."

Torosian glanced over at his team. "Polozov, you have your CDL license, don't you?"

"It's expired. But I still know how to drive one."

Torosian chuckled. "Like anyone will be checking any-more."

"Mine is still active," added Donnelly.

"Good. You two are on the salvage team."

"I'll lead it," offered Paul.

"Thanks, but it's my people. I should lead the group."

"You're needed here to help secure this compound."

Torosian hesitated, knowing Paul was right.

"Besides, we have a lot more experience in this than you do. Once we're supplied up, we'll be on our way."

"Are you sure?"

"Yes."

"I can't argue with that. How many people do you need?"

"Who on my team is going?"

Daphne, Ian, Ed, Lisa, and Akiko raised their hands.

"Akiko, I need you to stay here and keep an eye on the kids."

Akiko tensed up but maintained her composure, though it was obvious she was angry and disappointed. "Why am I always the one who has to babysit?"

"It's nothing personal. One of us has to stay behind to take care of the kids in case the rest of us don't make it back. You're the best one for the job."

"Is it because I'm the best one for the job, or because I don't handle myself well enough out there?"

Paul stepped over to Akiko and gently placed his hands on her upper arms, speaking in a quiet tone. "We all know you're not good at defending yourself. The reason I don't bring you along isn't because you're a danger to the team. You're a danger to yourself. I never want to have to tell Toshii his mother was killed by one of those things. I'd rather hurt your feelings than break his heart."

Akiko bowed her head a few inches. Thank you."

"Are we good?"

She forced a smile. "We're good."

Paul turned to Torosian. "I'll need twelve of your people."

"I'm in," said Heather. "You'll need me to show you around."

The husband stepped forward. "I'm Dan. My wife and I'll go."

The Asian woman beside him raised her hand. "I'm Ana-belle."

The woman who shut down Pam raised her hand. "Dawn Woolems. Count me in."

Eight others volunteered, six men and two women. When the team was chosen, Paul called them together.

"We're going to head out in ten minutes. Grab whatever you can find as a weapon."

"Are you expecting trouble?" asked Daniel.

"No, but better safe than sorry. We have a Honda Pilot, but we'll need three more vehicles."

Daniel and two others volunteered theirs.

"Thanks. We'll lead. Heather is with me since she knows how to get there. We'll meet at the cars in ten minutes.'

Chapter Two

PAUL AND HALF the team stood along the edge of the woods a hundred yards from the front of the FedEx facility. Donnelly led the other half in a slow circle around the exterior gate, hugging the tree line as they surveyed the sides and rear of the building. While Paul waited for them to return, he scanned the compound through his binoculars. Nothing wandered around out front, which was something to be grateful for.

"How does it look?" asked Daphne.

"No signs of deaders."

"Thank God for that."

Heather gestured toward the binoculars. "May I?"

"Be my guest."

Heather scanned the building. "Two trailers are backed up to the loading dock, which means they were in the middle of unloading when the shit hit the fan. That also means there'll be plenty of stuff to sort through. All the bay doors are shut, and the main gate is closed."

"What about the trailers parked outside the building?" asked Ed.

"The four trailers without cabs means they've been unloaded already. The fifth with the truck attached was probably waiting its turn when the staff abandoned the place. I don't see any bodies in the lot or signs the place has been ransacked." Heather handed the binoculars back to Paul. "I'll take that as a good sign."

"So do I."

"What about all those cars in the parking lot?" asked Ian.

"Maybe people left in groups for safety?" suggested Lisa.

"Or they're deaders roaming around inside," added Ed.

"Or they could be smart like us," said Polozov. "Maybe they stay where supplies are? Then we become bad guys for breaking in."

Paul shrugged. "We'll find out once we're inside."

Donnelly's team joined the others.

"What did you find?" asked Paul.

"Nothing. No deaders or bodies lying around, and no signs the place has been looted. All the doors are sealed tighter than my wife's cooch whenever I ask for sex."

Daphne chuckled.

"Did you see any trucks?" asked Heather.

"There's seven backed up to bays along the left side and one on the right."

"That's a good sign," said Heather. "If the trucks are there, the packages haven't been shipped out yet."

"Let's go see what it's like inside." Paul motioned for the others to follow. "Keep several feet apart in case someone is inside and armed."

"I'm right behind you," joked Daphne.

Paul led the way down to the access road and headed for the main gate, hoping that if anyone was inside, they would not mistake them for raiders and defend themselves. They had three firearms: his Vepr-12 semi-automatic shotgun and Daphne's Mossberg, with only thirteen rounds between them, and Ed's Glock 23, with only three rounds. Lisa carried her .357 Magnum and Ian his Colt 1911 semi-automatic pistol, though both were out of ammunition. They left the .38 with five rounds back at camp with Akiko. The others carried whatever they could find as weapons, everything from axes, crowbars, and tire irons to a baseball bat with nails hammered into the end. Paul realized this could quickly turn into a

Charlie Foxtrot. His people kept their firearms in the low-ready position to pose no immediate threat and kept their eyes focused on the building for any signs of trouble.

Once in the employee parking lot, Heather indicated for them to stop.

"Problem?" asked Paul.

"The opposite. The front gate is closed. If the place had been looted, I doubt they would have secured it behind them. Follow me."

Heather approached the employee's entrance to the security guard station. She and Paul made their way to the first window and looked inside. No bodies, no blood, no carnage.

Heather grinned. "Let's go."

The team passed through the turnstiles and gathered in the guard station. Ian, Ed, and Lisa checked the rooms off to the side for possible deaders, thankfully finding nothing that posed a threat.

Paul turned to the others. "Let me go first in case there's trouble."

"I'll do it," said Daphne.

"I need you to get the others out of here in case things go south and to lead the group."

"Okay," she answered reluctantly. "Be careful, hon."

Paul slung the Vepr over his shoulder and exited the station, his arms raised by his sides.

"Is anyone inside?"

No answer. Even better, no warning shot.

"We're not a raiding party, and we mean no one any harm. We'd like to barter with you if you have any supplies."

Still no response.

Paul reached the building without incident. He peered through the windows along the wall to his right. The lights still shone inside. The cubicle farm indicated this was the facility's office space. He pressed the buzzer to the door.

"Is anyone there?"

Still no response, which did not surprise him. This time, he rapped hard on the glass, expecting a horde of deaders to charge the window.

Silence.

Paul turned and waved for the others to join him.

Daphne reached him first and clasped his hand. "What now?"

"We go in."

Heather opened the door to the loading docks and stepped inside. Paul followed, motioning for the others to stay behind.

"Is anyone here?" called Heather.

No response.

"It's Heather. I used to work here."

Nothing.

Paul waved for the others to join them. Once they were all inside, he turned to Heather.

"This is your show. Where's the best place to start?"

Heather thought for a moment, then pointed to the rows of FedEx vans directly across from the entrance.

"They deliver to homes and small businesses. Most of the stuff won't be of use to us. But, if there's any food, prescription meds, and things like that, you'll find them in those trucks. Oh, the van in slot twenty-six is the one that makes deliveries to Costa Arms and The Gun Emporium, the local gun stores."

Daphne raised her hand. "Lisa and I will take that one."

"Thanks." Paul pointed to Daniel, his wife Annabelle, and two volunteers, Doug Dunnan and Trey Tumulty. "Help them go through the vans."

"How do we know what to look for?" asked Annabelle.

"Go by the return addresses," replied Heather. "If you think something might be useful, open it up."

"What should we do with anything we find?" asked Dunnan.

Paul hesitated, not sure how to respond.

"Just pile anything you find outside the vans," said

Heather. "I'll swing by with the carts later to pick them up and load them onto the trucks. The rest of you, follow me."

Heather crossed through the facility until they reached a conveyor belt that stretched from the front of the building, where the unloading bays were located to the rear wall. She paused.

"When the trucks are unloaded, the packages are thrown onto the conveyor. Smaller ones are diverted down there where they're sorted before being sent to the van." Heather pointed to a circular area with shelved bins. "Packages to be loaded onto the trailers are distributed via the overhead belts. The larger ones stay here and are either pulled off and sent to the vans or go down to the far end and are loaded onto the trailers."

"I'll sort through the small packages," said Hazi Gafford.

"Thanks." Heather led the others along the conveyor to the rear of the building. Ten bays sat on either side of the building. Six on the left were open with trailers backed up to them. The first was empty. Heather stopped. "We'll use this as the first truck. Who's driving?"

"We are." Polozov pointed to him and Donnelly.

Heather pointed to a door by the first bay. "That leads outside. Some of the drivers leave their keys in the ignition. See if the trucks in Bays One and Ten are ready to roll. If not, find ones that work and switch them out."

Polozov pointed his finger at her and made a clicking sound, then he and Donnelly headed outside.

Heather continued walking.

"Don't bother with Bay Three. It's computer chips and electronics for a tech manufacturer in Leesburg. Bay Four contains packages for Target, Walmart, and Auto Zone. They always get shipments of tires, which would be useful, plus cases of oil and transmission fluid."

"We'll check it out," said John Medugno. He gestured for Richard French to follow.

"Bay Seven is mostly Petco and PetSmart. He also delivers

to Firestone, so there'll be tires and auto supplies in there."

Ed tapped Dawn on the shoulder. "We'll take it."

"Grab a couple of cases of dog food for Gojira," suggested Paul.

"Roger that."

"Bay Nine is a hodgepodge of stores. The driver delivers to Reebok, so you should find some sneakers, running shoes, and socks there. He also delivers to Dicks, so there may be something useful there."

"Like baseball bats?" asked Johnny Thompson.

"Exactly. He also delivers to a Super Walmart, which often gets prescriptions mailed to them.

"My brother and I got it covered."

"How do you know all this?" asked Ian as they continued down the line.

"I used to work these trucks."

"Glad we found you. This will save us lots of time."

Paul pointed to the only open bin on the right. "What's in there?"

"Nothing useful. He delivers to the mall. "JC Penny, Macy's, Hobby Lobby, Spencer's, Bath and Body Works."

"We might find some useful clothes in there," suggested Dorrie Woods.

"I got that covered." Heather smiled and stopped in front of Bay Ten.

Paul peered inside. Piles of boxes for JoAnn's Fabrics and Game Stop lined the wall nearest the opening. "What good are these?"

"They're not. Check the back."

Paul stepped in to get a closer look. The front third of the trailer was packed with boxes for Bass Pro Shops.

"Sweet."

"What did I tell you?" Heather tapped the two piles of boxes near the end of the trailer. "Just pull these out and throw them to the side. We'll use this as the second truck."

"I got this covered," said Paul.

"I'll gather what we find so we can start loading up."

"Thanks. Ian, Dorrie, check the conveyer for anything that might be useful, then start loading the truck in Bay One."

"No problem." Ian and Dorrie headed off.

As Heather walked away, Paul stepped inside the trailer and grabbed the nearest package to offload. This was going better than he had hoped for.

DAPHNE AND LISA strolled through the loading area, looking for slot twenty-six. They reached the end of the first row and circled around to the second. Lisa pointed to the second van on the right.

"There it is."

The two women stepped up onto the platform and entered the rear compartment. Metal shelves lined the interior behind the driver's seat, the front filled with cardboard boxes. Ten boxes the length of longarms lay stacked behind the bulkhead. The women looked at each other, a gleam of hope in their expressions.

"Shit, I don't have a knife," said Daphne.

"Neither do I. Hang on." Lisa searched the shelves for a carton cutter. Not finding one, she entered the cab and rummaged around the dashboard and glove compartment. "Yes."

"What did you find?"

"A lock knife."

Lisa stepped back into the cargo area, pulled one of the long boxes onto the floor, slit the sealed tape, and opened the lid. An AK-47 semiautomatic rifle rested inside the box on a foam rubber surface.

"Sweet." Daphne lifted the Kalashnikov out of its bedding.

"Did you ever fire one of those?"

"No. But I will be soon."

Lisa pointed to the shelves behind Daphne and handed her the knife. "See if those contain ammo."

Daphne took the top package from the middle shelf, cut the tape sealing it shut, and opened the flaps. Inside sat twenty boxes, each containing fifty rounds of forty caliber ammunition, more than enough for the Glock.

Daphne smiled. "We hit the jackpot."

DANIEL STOOD IN front of his group, studying the vans and trucks. They had been backed in on either side of three smaller conveyor belts, eight vehicles per side. Small packages lay scattered across the floor or piled up at the end of the belts.

"This will take forever," complained Duggan.

"It shouldn't," Daniel responded. "Most of the packages will be of no use to us. As Heather said, check the return addresses. If it's from a person, ignore it. If it's from a company, open it only if you think it might be useful. And feel them if they're envelopes. If it's a bottle of pills, take it. Even if it's vitamins, we can use it."

"What do we do with them?" asked Dunnan.

Annabelle grabbed an empty plastic container from the floor and handed it to him. "Throw them in here. It'll make it easier to load."

Daniel clapped his hands. "Everybody grab a row and start sorting."

HAZI SORTED THROUGH the pile of small packages and envelopes quicker than anticipated, mostly because well over ninety-five percent of them came from private citizens or companies that did not sell anything of value for their survival. After the first ten minutes, she stopped reading the return addresses and switched to feeling through the packaging what was inside, only opening those that felt like they might contain something of value. Even using that method, she had set aside less than thirty parcels to bring back, most of which would probably be of little or no value.

She grabbed one unusually long box, almost two feet long and heavier than most others. Curiosity got the better of her. Hazi glanced around for something to open it, eventually finding a fountain pen. She used the tip to break the seals, then opened the lid and removed the packing material. Hazi rolled her eyes and mumbled, "For Christ's sake."

Inside the cardboard shipping container was a display box with a plastic view screen showing the contents—a 17.5-inch, deep brown, life-like fake penis with a suction cup on one end for hands-free use. The photo in the upper right corner showed a naked Asian lady holding the toy and smiling. Bold red letters on the bottom read Extra Large for Vaginal and Anal Pleasure.

"No wonder the apocalypse began."

Hazi threw it over her shoulder and resumed going through the remainder, hoping to find something more useful.

POLOZOV APPROACHED THE trailer sitting outside of Bay One. He crawled up the steps of the cab and peered inside. A keychain dangled from the ignition. The Russian gave Donnelly a thumbs up.

"The keys are there?"

"*Da.*"

"Start it and make sure it's working."

Polozov climbed into the cab, slid into the driver's seat, and turned the key. The engine turned over. He gave his friend another thumbs up.

"Let's check the truck in Bay Ten," said Donnelly.

Polozov shut down the engine and climbed out of the cab. The two men walked down the side of the building until they reached the last truck. Polozov opened the door and checked the ignition.

"*Der'mo.*"

"What's wrong?"

"No keys." The Russian pulled himself into the cab. He checked the dashboard, pulled down the visors, and felt around the floor and under the front seat.

"Any luck?"

"*Nyet.*"

Polozov checked the seat and floor on the passenger side. Finding nothing, he opened the glove compartment and rummaged through the contents. After a few seconds, he slammed shut the compartment lid.

"*Yebat'.*"

"No key?"

Polozov jumped onto the pavement and slammed shut the door.

"Calm down," urged Donnelly. "We'll check out the others. One of them has to have keys. We'll then switch it out with the truck in Bay Ten. Come on."

"Jesus," said French.

"What?" Medugno did not look up as he separated the boxes for AutoZone.

"There's twenty-seven tires piled up in here."

"So? Where do you think auto shops get their tires? The tire stork?"

French either ignored the insult or didn't catch it. "That's a lot to unstack."

"For Christ's sake," mumbled Medugno. He shoved the case of motor oil he was carrying against French's chest. "You take care of this shit. I'll handle the tires."

French took the box and groaned. "This is heavy."

Medugno shook his head. Pulling a tire off the top of the stack, he placed it on the floor and rolled it into the building.

ED SORTED THROUGH the piles of boxes for Petco and PetSmart first, setting aside four large cases of dog food. He then quickly checked the stacks for the other stores on the off chance there might be something useful there. As expected, he found nothing.

Turning around to check on Dawn, he did not see her. For a moment, Ed wondered if she had decided to slack off, or worse, if a deader they had missed had taken her out. Unholstering his Glock, Ed headed for the end of the trailer to search for her, pausing when Dawn rounded the corner and passed by him.

"Where have you been?"

Dawn motioned with her head to the stack of tires piled against the trailer wall across from him. "I've been moving them down to Bay One."

Ed glanced over his shoulder, immediately feeling embarrassed. Of the fifteen tires originally inside, she had already moved more than half of them into the other trailer.

"Sorry. I didn't mean to imply—"

Dawn waved her hand, cutting him off. "No offense taken. But can I offer a suggestion?"

"Sure."

She pointed to the four cases of dog food. "Don't feed that stuff to your dog. It's as bad as fast food."

"What should I feed him?"

Dawn pulled a tire from the top of the stack and rolled it over to Ed. "You finish transferring these. I'll find something good for him."

"SHIT," SIGHED JOHNNY. "There has to be at least a hundred boxes for Reebok. How am I going to go through them all?"

"You're not," answered Joey as he sorted through the stack placed aside for Dick's.

Johnny stared at his brother as if he had just joined the

ranks of the living dead.

"There's thirty people at the campsite, plus the newcomers. And we have no idea what everyone's shoe size is. We'll load them all into the trailer and take them with us."

"Good idea."

"Of course, it is. That's why I'm your smarter older brother."

"But I got the looks.

Joey flipped his brother the middle finger. "Go through the Walmart stuff for anything useful while I sort through this."

Johnny obliged. After a few minutes, he called out, "Friggin' A."

"What did you find?"

Johnny held up a box and faced the front to his brother, showing a Mr. Coffee twelve-cup coffee maker.

"Like that'll save us from deaders."

"No, but at least we can enjoy ourselves between attacks."

Joey started to argue but thought better of it. As their old man used to say, it's the little things in life that count the most.

"Put it with the rest of the stuff. We'll take it if we find any coffee to go with it."

IAN AND DORRIE made their way along the conveyor until they reached Heather in the middle. She stood by a cart with four three-sided cages on wheels linked to it.

"What's that?" asked Ian.

"We use it to bring heavy and oversized items to the vans." She pulled a set of gold clubs off one of the carts and laid it against the conveyor. "Did you find anything?"

"A lot," said Dorrie. "A picnic table that needs assembling, sleeping bags, and folding lawn chairs. But they're too big to carry."

"No problem. Stand back."

Ian and Dorrie moved away. Heather pressed a red button

on a console beneath the frame. The belt started moving.

"This will take everything to the end," Heather yelled to be heard over the noise. "We'll load them onto the last truck later. Dorrie, stay here and help me. Ian, there are two trucks at the other end of the building. They may not have been unloaded yet. Check them out."

"Okay." Ian made his way to the bay doors.

"What do you want me to do?" asked Dorrie.

Heather handed her a black magic marker from off the workbench. "Place an X on anything we can use. It'll make it easier to load later."

"I DON'T BELIEVE this," said Dunnan as he stood outside one of the vans.

"What?" asked Tumulty from the van opposite him.

Dunnan pulled out a kayak and dropped it in the aisle. "Who orders one of these by mail?"

"Who cares? Just leave it and search for stuff that's useful."

HAZI WENT THROUGH the last of the bins. She had found several bottles of medicine and a set of insulin injections packed in ice. The older guy with diabetes would be pleased. She should be finished in a few minutes.

POLOZOV CHECKED THE truck of the trailer parked in Bay Nine.

"Yahtzee."

"What?" asked Donnelly.

"Isn't that what Americans say when they win?"

"You mean Bingo."

"Whatever. This one has keys."

"Good. Start her up. I'll uncouple it from the trailer."

IAN STOOD IN front of the two loading docks. The bay and trailer doors to the right were open, showing the back half-filled with packages. Since nothing had been sorted, it would take a while to go through them all. The one to its left had the inner door open, but the sliding door to the trailer was closed and secured. Hopefully, that one was already unloaded and would be easier to start with. Ian stepped over to it, undid the latch, and started to raise the door.

The stench of rotting flesh flowed out along with the groans of the living dead. Ian tried to slam down the sliding door when several decayed hands grabbed the bottom and lifted, exposing close to a hundred deaders that had been trapped inside.

Chapter Three

IAN DID NOT stand a chance.

A deader in a security guard uniform surged out and grabbed Ian by the collar, holding him in place. Ian kept his hand close to his chest and swung his right elbow, catching the deader on the side of its head and disconnecting the jaw. The mandible dangled at an awkward angle, flapping around as the thing tried to bite him. Ian raised his right leg and kicked it back into the away.

Two more deaders tackled him from each side and dragged him to the floor. Ian rolled to one side, breaking the grip of the deader on his right as he rolled closer to the one on the left. The latter leaned forward, sinking its rotting teeth into Ian's cheek and tearing away a chunk of skin and muscle. Too panicked to cry out, Ian broke away from the deader munching on his flesh and scrambled to his feet, only to be brought down by five more living dead. They rolled the teenager onto his back. Four of them dug their rotting hands into his abdomen, pulling away the skin and grasping for organs. One tore out his stomach and bit into it, bursting the organ. Stomach acid splashed across Ian's face. The fifth, a female deader with the top half of its face ripped off, grabbed his intestines and began unwinding them, frantically shoving the food into its mouth.

Four living dead dropped to their knees, pushing aside those already feasting, ravaging what was left. Those that could not get close enough to the body settled for arms and legs, chewing chunks of muscle and skin off Ian's limbs as if they

21

were barbecued chicken wings.

Ian screamed at the top of his lungs, the cry starting as one of pain and terror and quickly devolving into madness as the last bits of his sanity were consumed along with his flesh. The screaming died out within seconds, echoing off the walls, accompanied by the deaders' snarling.

Those unable to feast on Ian swarmed into the facility seeking other prey, half following the conveyor belt down to the loading bays, the other half flowing across the floor toward the rows of vans.

HAZI HEARD THE moaning of the living dead, followed moments later by Ian's death cries. She leaned back and peered through the stacks of plastic bins, her eyes widening in fear at the sight of nearly a hundred deaders swarming from the unloading dock into the facility. They had not spotted her yet, hopefully. Yet they were close enough that if she tried to run, they would see her and give chase. She had only one chance, as shitty as it was.

Moving to the back of the area, Hazi crouched down and hoped none of the living dead would notice her.

LISA'S HEAD SHOT up, and she stared at the rear of the van. "Did you hear that?"

"What?"

Lisa placed a finger across her lips.

A second later, the snarls of rampaging deaders flowed through the building.

Daphne rushed over to the stacked boxes of ammo and began rummaging through it for shotgun shells.

"Lisa, what are you carrying?"

"The Magnum. But it's out of rounds."

Daphne grabbed two boxes of .357 rounds and handed

them to Lisa, then slid two boxes of shotgun shells into her jacket pockets. She moved to the rear of the van, crouched down, and intertwined the fingers of her hand.

"Get on the roof. We'll be safe up there."

Lisa did not have to be told twice. She used Daphne's hands as a foothold to climb onto the van's roof, then turned and helped her friend up.

DANIEL HEARD THE approaching horde and rushed out of the van he was searching through. He did not see any deaders but did spot Daphne and Lisa climbing onto the van's roof in Slot Twenty-Six.

Annabel emerged from the van two slots down on the opposite side, searching frantically for him.

"Stay there," he called.

Daniel vaulted over the rollers and rushed up to his wife.

"Are those deaders?"

"Yes." Daniel grabbed his wife by the arms and pushed her into the van. "We'll be safer in here."

Annabel screamed. Daniel turned as a dozen deaders entered the space between the two rows of vans and surged toward him.

THREE VANS DOWN from Slot Twenty-six, Dunnan heard the commotion from the other end of the facility.

Tumulty stepped out of the opposite van, clutching a container of bottled water. He was about to ask his friend where the noise came from but stopped, following Tumulty's gaze to the end of the line.

Eleven deaders appeared at the end of the row and rushed toward them on either side of the rollers.

THE COMMOTION AT the far end of the facility caught Heather's attention. Leaning over the conveyor belt, she spotted the horde surging from the trailer and spreading out across the facility.

"Fuck."

"What?" Dorrie followed the woman's gaze, shocked by the sight of so many deaders.

Upon seeing them, a dozen deaders set off along the belt, drawing dangerously close. Heather slammed her hand against the red power button, shutting down the belt. The sudden stop knocked the deaders off balance, buying them a few seconds.

Heather directed Dorrie toward the caged cargo transport directly behind the cart.

"What are you doing?"

"You'll be safe in there." Heather slid into the driver's seat of the cart. "And grab a weapon."

Dorrie tossed the bag of golf clubs into the transport.

Heather pulled away from the conveyor as the first deaders reached them.

MEDUGNO WAS ROLLING two tires on either side of him when screams and snarls echoed from the other side of the facility. He pushed the tires down toward Bay One. As they bounced off the wall and fell onto the floor, Medugno moved out to the center aisle to see what caused the commotion.

Scores of the living dead swarmed along the conveyor, many breaking away from the main pack and heading into the other part of the facility. The deader at the head of the pack, a large man with its right arm stripped of flesh down to the bone, spotted Medugno and raced toward him. Its snarling attracted others. Soon, several dozen of the living dead rushed toward him.

Medugno stepped back slowly, considering his options.

"We got trouble," he tried to warn his friend.

French did not respond. Medugno considered dropping back to warn him but knew that would only get both of them killed. Instead, he opted for self-preservation and bolted for the door beside Bay One leading outside. With luck, the things would follow and get clogged at the exit, giving him and French a chance to escape.

Medugno pushed his way through the door and nearly fell down the stairs. The pack of deaders was only a few yards behind.

JOHNNY DRAGGED A box with an inflatable mattress to the end of the trailer, pushed it over the dock board into the facility, and stacked it by the rollers. He noticed Medugno eight bays down staring into the facility before suddenly heading for the exit. A few seconds later, a pack of deaders rounded the corner and followed. Johnny crouched, hoping the things would not spot him.

Joey stepped onto the platform. "Quit screwing around. We got a lot of shit to sort through."

"Shit," Johnny mumbled.

Joey's comment caught the attention of nine of the living dead. Swerving away from the rest of the pack, the nine deaders rushed down the bays, jumping over the gravity roller conveyor belt and rushing the two brothers.

PAUL KNEW THE sound all too well but hoped to hell he was wrong. Making his way to the end of the trailer, he leaned forward and peered around the corner, cursing under his breath as he saw the pack drawing closer.

DANIEL SLID INTO the back of the van and crouched, sliding down the door. Dead hands slapped against the metal, the sound made more intimidating by the snarling and moaning for food.

Daniel could not close it completely because a foot in a heavy work boot stood on the threshold. He raised the door a few inches and slammed the edge against its toes but, because of the steel-toed boots, and probably the fact the thing felt no pain, it did not budge. If any of the deaders were smart enough to reach down and lift the door, he and Annabelle would be joining those outside.

He glanced over his shoulder at Annabelle. Daniel motioned to the foot. "Push that back so I can close the door."

Annabelle pulled out the two-wheel hand cart resting against the van's interior, placed the nose plate against the deader's foot, and used her heel to shove the two-wheeler forward. The nose plate pushed the foot outside. The door slammed shut. Daniel secured the latch, stood, and hugged his wife.

The sound of dead hands slapping the left side of the van echoed inside. Daniel scanned the cab.

"Shit. The driver's door is open."

Annabelle ran forward, leaned over the driver's seat, and reached over to shut the door.

A deader with no jaw and half its face eaten away centered itself in the doorway, making a gurgling sound. Annabelle kicked it in the face, fracturing the front part of its skull. The deader stumbled back, tripped over a box, and fell against the rollers. Before Annabelle could close the door, a female deader covered in blood, a huge chunk ripped out of its neck, jumped into the driver's seat, knocking Annabelle over. She placed her hands on its shoulders and pushed up, keeping it from getting to her.

Daniel picked up the two-wheeler, holding it by the handle and frame, and rushed forward.

"Hey, asshole."

The female deader turned to him and snarled.

Using all his strength, Daniel slammed the nose plate into the deader's face, cleaving its head in half. Annabelle kicked the body off her. It fell back, collapsing into a crumbled heap outside the van. Annabelle slammed shut the door and locked it seconds before a third deader reached the driver's side. It bit at the window and tried to claw its way in, leaving bloody handprints on the glass. Annabel retreated to the rear of the van.

Daniel massaged his right shoulder.

"Are you hurt?"

"I just threw out a muscle lifting that thing. What about you? Did it bite you?"

"Thank God, no. What do we do now?"

"We have to wait until someone comes for us."

The two hugged each other tightly, waiting for the end.

DUNNAN KNEW HE would never get out of this alive, but at least he might be able to buy time for Tumulty. With no other options available, he lifted the kayak by the rim of the cockpit and held it horizontally across his chest.

"Go find some cover," he yelled.

"What about you?" asked Tumulty.

"I got you covered."

Dunnan charged into the pack, ramming the keel into the deaders. Two were shoved against the rollers and thrown over to the other side. Three were knocked to the left, tumbling between the vans. The rest were pushed to the floor, tripping Dunnan. He fell forward, his chest crashing into the kayak. The man cried out as two of his ribs fractured.

The pain in his chest lasted only a few seconds, replaced by agony as the deaders sunk their teeth into Dunnan's legs, ripping off chunks of flesh. He tried to break free, but there were too many. For every set of hands he kicked away, two more grabbed him. Dunnan thrashed about, punching the deaders or kicking at them, to no avail. The five deaders to the sides crawled back, joining the others in tearing apart Dunnan. He fought back as long as possible until the pain and loss of blood overcame him. Dunnan slowly slipped into unconsciousness, followed by death.

Tumulty stood frozen in place, too shocked to move.

"Over here," yelled a female voice.

At first, he did not respond.

"Hey. Up here."

Tumulty glanced up to see Lisa crouching on top of the van in Slot Twenty-Six, holding her hand out to him.

"Hurry up if you want to live."

LISA WAS HELPING Tumulty onto the roof of the FedEx van when a deader ten feet away lunged at him. Daphne fired two rounds at the thing. The first tore open its chest, slowing it. The second struck its face, blowing off the front of its head. It dropped to the platform, tripping those behind it, which gave Lisa enough time to lift Tumulty to safety.

"Thanks." Tumulty paused to catch his breath. "I'd be dead if it wasn't for you."

"Don't count that out yet." Daphne pumped several shotgun rounds into the pile of deaders struggling to their feet. "Unless we clear out this place, we're stuck up here."

"What are we waiting for?" Lisa picked up the Magnum from the roof and fired at a deader with no right arm at the side of the van. Its head erupted, splattering the side in gore.

"Do you have another gun?" asked Tumulty.

Daphne shook her head. "If you want to help, attract them to us."

"Are you nuts?"

"We can't kill them if we can't see them."

Tumulty repeatedly stomped his foot and shouted, attracting the attention of the living dead in the other aisles. As they raced toward the van, Daphne and Lisa took them down one by one.

WHEN THE HORDE had passed, Hazi stood and made her way to the exit. A deader with a broken ankle limped by. On seeing her, it rushed up the three stairs to feed. Hazi grabbed the only weapon she had available and smashed the tip of the 17.5-inch black dildo against its head. The deader paused, momentarily stunned, then snarled and headed back up.

Hazi shoved the tip of the dildo into the thing's decaying mouth and pushed, driving half of it down the deader's throat. It gagged and bit down on the sex toy, shattering half a dozen rotten teeth. The deader grabbed the end of the dildo, trying to pull it out, but the tip was too deeply lodged in its throat. It thrashed about, unsure how to respond.

Seizing the opportunity, Hazi raced down the stairs, shoving the thing aside, and ran for the vans.

MEDUGNO BOUND DOWN the steps into the parking lot, pausing long enough to frantically search for a place to hide or a means of escape. A truck engine started off to his right. He turned in that direction, spotting Polozov and Donnelly by Bay Nine.

The door Medugno had come through slammed open and seven deaders rushed out of the facility, bolting down the stairs and racing across the lot.

Medugno broke into a run and headed toward the two men, waving his arms and yelling to get their attention.

DONNELLY HAD STARTED to detach the trailer when he heard Medugno from across the parking lot. He turned to see what was happening, wondering why he was running from....

The seven deaders chasing behind Medugno answered the question.

Donnelly stepped up to the cab and pounded on the door.

Polozov leaned out the window. "Is trailer detached?"

Donnelly pointed to the living dead. "We have problems."

"*Yebat'.*"

Both men watched the deaders catch up with Medugno. The smallest of the pack, and as such the fastest, leaped onto Medugno's back, digging its teeth into his neck and tackling him to the pavement. The others dove in, biting into limbs or tearing off chunks of flesh. Medugno screamed and fought back, both actions slowly decreasing in intensity until he stopped moving. The deaders devoured his remains.

"Get in," said Polozov.

Donnelly ran around the front of the cab and crawled into the passenger's seat. "Are we running?"

"Fuck no. We are to play… how do you Americans call it? *Da*, bumper cars with the dead."

IN BAY NINE, Johnny stared at the approaching horde. A topless male deader, most of the skin and muscles in its chest and upper arms chewed away, spotted him and broke away. Eight others followed.

Joey rushed up and pushed Johnny to one side.

"Close the fucking door."

Joey grabbed the handle and pulled it down. The door slid halfway down the rollers and stopped, the edge catching on a large box containing a patio table. The brothers tried to shove the box out of the way, only to find it caught on the dock board.

The truck lurched forward and pulled away from the load-ing dock. The shirtless deader jumped the gap, its upper body landing in the trailer. One arm scratched at the wooden floor while the other grasped Joey's left ankle, knocking him over backward. Joey raised his right leg and repeatedly kicked the deader in the face. Each blow did damage—knocking out teeth, tearing off its nose, crushing its left eye—but the thing would not let go.

Johnny grabbed a box containing a microwave oven and slammed it against the deader's face. The force of the impact made it lose its grip. It slid out of the truck and onto the pavement. Johnny chucked the box at its head. The corner caught the deader in the right eye, crushing its head.

Johhny climbed to his feet. "Thanks."

"Don't thank me yet." Johnny pointed to the loading dock.

The other eight deaders fell off into the parking lot, crawled back to their feet, and gave chase.

FRENCH STACKED THE fourth box of motor oil in the center of the aisle as snarling came from the loading dock. Four deaders rushed toward him. He picked up the box of motor oil and threw it at the lead deader, a female with heavily tattooed arms and long brunette hair matted in blood. It knocked the box out of the way and lunged, catching French in the stomach and toppling him over. French's head hit the corner of a wooden pallet, rendering him unconscious, a lucky break for him since he never felt the living dead pile on top of him and tear out his intestines and organs.

ED COULD TELL by the commotion that deaders were loose in the facility. He raced to the end of the trailer, hoping he was not too late.

"Dawn, get in here where it's safe."

Dawn had already spotted the approaching danger. The closest was only a few yards away. Knowing that running would be futile, she lifted the tire off the top of the stack and chucked it at the deader. The tire caught it in the face, bouncing off to one side and knocking the thing back against the next two in line. The three collapsed in a heap, slowing the others.

Four more raced down the conveyor belt. Dawn reached down and pressed the red emergency stop button. The belt started, throwing the deaders off balance. One fell over on the other side of the conveyor. The other three stumbled and fell. Dawn used the opportunity to run for the trailer.

She did not see the deader vault over the rollers behind her and close in for the kill.

Ed did. He grabbed a nearby tire and ran to help her.

"Move aside."

Dawn dodged to her right as the thing lunged, missing her by inches. Ed rushed forward and dropped the tire over the deader's head, pushing down on the rubber so it locked its shoulders in place. The deader slammed into Ed. Both fell over. The tire struck Ed in the chest, knocking the wind out of him. Rolling to the side, the deader landed on its back. It tried to get at Ed but could not move because of the tire wrapped around its upper body, succeeding only in swaying back and forth.

Dawn rushed over to Ed and attempted to help him to his feet, but he was still groggy from the fall. Thankfully, someone further down the facility was creating noise, attracting the living dead away from them. She lifted Ed off the floor and leaned him against the rollers.

"Are you okay to walk?"

Ed nodded. "Get in the truck where you'll be safe."

"Not without you." Dawn wrapped Ed's right arm over her shoulders and led him back to the trailer.

PAUL SAW THE horde flowing through the facility, breaking off to go after others in the group. No one had firearms except for him and Daphne, and they only had thirteen rounds between them. This would be a slaughter.

Moving to the end of the rack of rollers between the conveyor belt and his trailer, Paul stood in the open so he could be seen and banged the stock of the Vepr against the metal. Three deaders stopped, looking around for the noise. Paul continued banging.

"Hey, meat sacks. You want a hot meal?"

The three deaders homed in on his voice and charged. Five more followed.

Eight in total.

And he had only seven shells.

Paul lined up on the nearest deader, a middle-aged woman that still clutched a scanner in her left hand. When ten feet away, Paul fired. The deader's head exploded in a cloud of gore. Paul checked behind him to make certain nothing blocked him, then slowly fell back, giving him a few added seconds to carefully aim and ensure headshots. The next six deaders went down with a single round each.

The eighth deader quickly limped toward him, its left foot missing and half the flesh chewed off the lower leg. Muscles and tight abs bulged beneath its blood-soaked t-shirt.

"This ain't my lucky day."

Paul raised his shotgun, surged forward, and rammed the stock as hard as he could into the muscular deader's face, followed by a loud crack. The blow caved in its left eye socket and ripped away the nose but did not slow it down. It grabbed the Vepr from Paul's hands and tossed it over the rollers. Paul retreated, keeping his focus on the thing. The deader lunged. Its left arm grasped Paul's shoulder while its right clutched his hair and yanked his head to the side, exposing his neck. The thing lowered its head to feed.

HEATHER PULLED AWAY from the conveyor belt and steered left, heading for the area where the vans were parked. Half a dozen deaders followed. One ran alongside the cages, its gaze fixed on Dorrie.

Dorrie removed a golf club from its carrier and slammed the head down on the deader's head. It staggered but continued pursuing them. She raised the club and brought it down even harder. Its skull caved in. The deader wobbled and fell. Its left hand grabbed one of the bars of the cage, hanging on relentlessly as its body was dragged along beside the carts. Dorrie rammed the club against its hand, breaking enough fingers that the deader let go and rolled to one side.

A second deader jumped onto the cage behind Dorrie and climbed up the bars until the upper half of its body protruded over the top. It snarled at her.

At that moment, the cart passed beneath the overhead conveyor belt. The steel frame slammed into its skull, snapping its spine and pushing the head at a ninety-degree angle. The deader held on for several seconds before dropping off onto the cement floor.

Dorrie breathed a sigh of relief until the cart entered the van loading area. Every deader nearby, thirty-seven in total, spotted the food driving around the facility and ran after it, leaving behind those trapped inside or on the vans.

"WHY ARE THEY leaving?" asked Lisa.

Tumulty pointed to the cart. "They're going after that."

The cart circled in front of the line of vans. Daphne fired a round into the air, catching the driver's attention.

"Come around again," yelled Daphne. She circled the index finger of her right hand over her head, then lifted the Mossberg.

The driver gave her a thumbs up.

"Lisa, climb onto one of the vans on the last line. Shoot as many of those things as possible when she comes by. Tumulty, you go with her."

"What are you going to do?"

"I'm going to wait on the other side and take out as many of those things as possible when they return."

DAN GREW AGITATED inside the van. Not because of the deaders outside, but because the gunfire echoing throughout the facility told him a battle between the living and living dead raged, and he couldn't be a part of it. Most of the deaders around their van broke away and rushed off after easier prey. A few still pounded on the doors, hoping to get at the food inside.

He stopped comforting Annabelle and rummaged through the back of the van.

"What are you looking for?" she asked.

"A weapon."

Annabelle's voice wobbled slightly. "Why?"

"I have to help the others."

"You won't make it past the loading dock."

The pounding of dead hands on the side of the van snapped Dan back to reality. Any attempt to get out would add him to the pack of deaders attacking his friends and put Annabelle at risk.

Dan punched one of the boxes in anger, then went back and comforted his wife.

DONNELLY LEANED FORWARD and looked out the passenger side window.

"We have more of those things following us. They're coming from inside the building."

Polozov did not respond. He drove until he reached the chain link fence at the far end of the compound and stopped. The Russian checked his side mirrors. The living dead were directly behind him and approaching fast.

"Great," protested Donnelly. "Now we're trapped."

"Trust in Russian ingenuity."

Polozov shifted into reverse.

JOHNNY AND JOEY tossed packages of non-essential items off the trailer, hoping to either take down or trip the pack following them. One deader got near the left side of the trailer. Joey waited until it was close, then flipped the glass lawn table off the end. The box fell on its head, crushing its skull. It collapsed into a bloody heap on the pavement.

The truck suddenly stopped, knocking the brothers off balance.

"What the fuck now?" asked Johnny.

Joey reached up to close the door so the living dead could not get to them.

The shrillness of the backup alarm cut through the compound, drowning out the sounds of the approaching pack. The trailer lurched into reverse, heading directly for the living dead.

One deader ran into the rear of the trailer, desperately clawing at the wood to get inside. After a few seconds, it lost its grip and slid under the vehicle.

The trailer swerved slightly to the right into an overweight deader with chunks of flesh hanging from its mouth, catching it with the left set of tires. The trailer hitched to one side as it rolled over the bloated body. A loud pop occurred as the deader exploded under the weight. A spray of blood and crushed organs shot across the ground. A moment later, the stench of decayed bodily fluids wafted through the floorboards.

Johnny fell to his knees and vomited.

Joey lost count of how many of the living dead were crushed over the next minute, but it had to be at least a dozen or more based on the amount of gore being splattered across the ground and the overpowering stench filling the trailer.

When they neared the wall of the facility, the truck finally stopped.

"Thank God," hacked Johnny, who had puked at least six times during the melee. "Let's get out of here."

Before he could dismount, the truck moved forward again.

Joey stared at his brother. "Now what?"

DONNELLY STARED OUT the windshield at the killing field, barely able to stomach the sight.

Fifteen of the living dead lay scattered around the lot, their crushed bodies having vomited out internal organs and congealed blood across the pavement. Only those whose heads had been flattened remained motionless. The others flailed their arms, groaning in desperation. One had its legs crushed, its arms dragging the mangled body toward the food. A second had its right leg mangled yet still stumbled across the lot.

"Let's finish job, *da?*"

Before Donnelly could answer, Polozov accelerated.

He steered into the stumbling deader first, knocking it over with the right front tire, popping it like an over-stuffed tick. Slowly maneuvering through the lot, the Russian crushed the living dead still remaining. Once on the other side of the carnage, he shifted into PARK and opened the door.

Donnelly stared at him. "Are you nuts?"

"What? There no danger from what's left." Polozov slid out. "Besides, I keep engine running. Come on."

Sighing in frustration, Donnelly exited the cab and joined the Russian. Polozov stood staring into the trailer, a confused look on his face.

"What are you doing in there?"

Joey moved to the end of the trailer and jumped off. "We were in back sorting packages when you drove off."

"Sorry."

"Don't be." Johnny joined them. "Those things would have gotten us if you hadn't pulled away when you did."

Polozov glanced into the back, noticing the pools of vomit.

"You two made a mess."

"*We* made a mess?" Joey pointed to the rear of the trailer. The undercarriage and tires dripped with congealed blood and chunks of flesh and organs. "What do you call this?"

"Deader killing, proper Russian style." Polozov's gaze focused on the rear set of tires on the left. He reached over and yanked something free, then showed a severed arm to the others. "See, I deserve a hand."

HAZI MADE HER way to a set of walls separating the office space from the warehouse. She leaned against the opening of a space that contained maintenance equipment, pausing to catch her breath and figure out her next course of action.

A commotion to her left caught Hazi's attention. Making her way down and peering around the corner, she watched as Heather drove a cage cart around the shipping area, attracting those deaders crowding around the vans, which then gave chase. She leaned back against the wall, praying none of the living dead would notice her and attack, feeling relieved only when the cart had passed with all the deaders in pursuit.

A noise that sounded like a cross between a snarl and a gargle made Hazi turn back toward the conveyor. The deader that had attacked her earlier staggered toward her, only a yard away, the dildo still lodged in its throat. With only a second to react, Hazi dodged to one side.

The deader hit the wall. It tried to stumble back to go after Hazi but could not, the suction cup on the base of the dildo having stuck to the wall. It tried to back away, but the sex toy was lodged too deeply down its throat. It could only thrash its arms around in frustration.

Hazi stared at the immobilized deader and mumbled, "You gotta be fucking kidding."

Glancing around, she spotted a metal toolbox on the floor outside the maintenance area. She picked it up. The toolbox

THE CHRONICLES OF PAUL III

was heavy, but not enough to prevent her from lifting it.

Hazi brought it over to the deader and smashed it against the back of its head. Its skull fractured. Pieces of broken bone and brain dropped through the wound onto the floor. Yet the damn thing kept moving. Raising it again, she used all her strength and slammed the toolbox against its head again. This time, the corner struck, crushing its skull and brain. The force of the blow pushed the remainder of the head forward until the entire dildo was lodged down its throat, still attached to the wall, and the body hanging by it.

Hazi shook her head. No one would believe her when she told them what happened.

PAUL'S ASS BACKED into something, knocking him over and throwing off the deader's aim. Its teeth snapped shut where his neck should have been, missing him by inches. Paul raised his left leg, placed his foot on the thing's chest, and kicked out, shoving it back a few feet.

Something underneath Paul was moving him away from the deader. He glanced around. He had backed into a second conveyor belt that carried misplaced packages to the overhead system. Not wanting to be caught up there, he stood and was about to run back to the end when the deader crawled onto the belt, blocking his path.

Paul turned and scrambled up the conveyor. The deader climbed to its feet and chased after him.

LISA AND TUMULTY made their way to the last line of vans, carefully searching the area for stray deaders that may not have joined the chasing horde.

"Which one do you want?" asked Tumulty.

Lisa chose one in the middle. Tumulty helped her up, then joined her. Lisa knelt near the edge, placed five boxes of .357

rounds in front of her, and reloaded the Magnum.

"What now?"

Lisa slid in the last round and closed the chamber. "We wait for Heather to come around."

DAPHNE CLIMBED OFF the van, landing in the only clear space not filled with the twenty-one corpses she and Lisa had taken down. As she made her way through the mass, one deader with half its head shot away reached up for her, snapping its teeth. She ignored it and made her way to the end of the line.

Across from her stood a ten-foot-square cage made of parts of a chain-link fence used for storing expensive items or materials that needed to be stored separately. It would make an ideal shooting position. She ran over to it. Thankfully, the padlock had not been secured. Daphne went inside, closed and secured the gate, and waited.

HEATHER DROVE BY the conveyor belt and turned left to circle back to the vans.

Dorrie kept her eyes on the last two carts. Three deaders climbed up the bars. She hoped they would not get this far.

Another of the living dead ran up alongside the first cage, reaching for Dorrie. She smashed the shaft of the golf club on its head. The skull cracked but did not slow the deader. Dorrie rammed the clubhead into its face, shattering several teeth and gouging out its left eye. The wounds still did not slow it down. When the deader lunged at Dorrie, she jammed the clubhead into its mouth, shoved it back, and released her grip. The deader swerved to the right and ran into a steel girder. The hard surface pushed the golf club through the deader's head until the clubhead erupted out of the back of its skull. It dropped to the floor.

More than thirty of the things still followed the cart.

PAUL HAD NEARLY made it to the top of the conveyor. He looked up in time to see a steel beam stretching across the facility less than a yard from him. Paul ducked, throwing himself off balance. He dropped to his knees, fearing this would be the end.

The deader did not notice the beam and ran into it face first, breaking its nose. It toppled over backward, laying on the conveyor, rolling from side to side, and groaning.

Paul chuckled at the sight. His merriment quickly changed when a metal bar hit him on the shoulders, diverting him off the main belt onto a smaller one leading to Bay Seven. The bar also sent the deader in his direction.

Shit.

He turned to see what waited for him at the end of the belt, and his heart sank.

DAWN WAS HELPING Ed to the trailer when the deader with the tire lodged around its arms climbed to its feet and charged. It crashed into Dawn, pushing her forward. She hit the cement wall headfirst, knocking her unconscious.

The deader switched its attention to Ed and rushed him. Still groggy from the blow to the head, Ed had barely turned to defend himself when the deader collided into him. The two stumbled back into the trailer, stopping only when they hit a stack of boxes once destined for Payless. Ed tried to raise his arms to push it away, but they were pinned by the tire. The deader snapped at him, its teeth inches away from Ed's face.

Dawn came to in time to see the attack. Using the wall as support, she staggered to her feet and rushed over to Ed. When she grabbed the tire and yanked the deader off Ed, it fell back, allowing the tire to slide off its arms. Ed slid to the floor. Caught off balance, Dawn stumbled back and tripped.

The deader turned away from Ed and attacked Dawn, pouncing on the woman and pinning her to the floor. She placed one hand on its chest and one on its chin and tried to push it away. The hand on its chin slipped on the gore-covered skin. Dawn's hand fell into the deader's mouth. It snapped its jaws shut, biting off her index and middle fingers. Dawn screamed and yanked her hand away, staring at the twin stumps that gushed blood.

Spitting out the fingers, the deader leaned forward and sunk its teeth into Dawn's neck. She felt them slice through the flesh into her larynx. The agony was unbearable. Dawn screamed in both pain and terror until the deader yanked its head back, tearing out her throat and severing her carotid artery. Her cries turned into a gurgle as blood flowed down her throat and into her lungs. Dawn drowned in her own blood.

Ed staggered to his feet. He looked around for a weapon but could not find any. He needed to do something before the thing finished feeding off Dawn and came after him. Stumbling over to the deader, Ed used both arms to put the thing in a headlock, then tried to snap its neck. Before he could, the deader became frantic, throwing itself from left to right, trying to break loose. Ed held on tight, knowing he could only maintain his grip for a few seconds at most.

"Here it comes."

Lisa raised the Magnum, knowing it would be difficult to get a headshot against moving targets from this distance. Of the three crawling onto the cart, she centered on the deader closest to Dorrie and pulled the trigger. Her aim was off, the round punching into the neck of the deader in the center. It fell off the cart and landed on its back. Lisa lined up a second shot but paused. The deader lay motionless from the waist down, the bullet having severed its spine. All it could do was reach up and snarl. Lisa switched aim to the last deader on the cart.

"Damn, you're good," said Tumulty. "You nailed that son of a bitch in its spine."

"I was aiming for the head of the one in front of it."

"Oh." Tumulty sounded disappointed.

Lisa fired. The round caught the deader in its left arm, tearing it apart above the elbow. The thing still held on with its right hand, swinging back and forth. Lisa adjusted her aim and fired two more rounds. The first passed in front of its face. The second caught it in the left temple, blasting off the top half of its head. The deader toppled off the cart, tripping up two of the living dead following behind.

Swinging the revolver toward the pack, she fired off the last three rounds in rapid succession. All of them hit their mark, but only one caused a head wound that brought down the deader.

Lisa swung open the cylinder, emptied the spent shell casings, and reloaded.

"Shit," said Tumulty.

Lisa raised her head. Seven of the living dead had broken away from the chase and headed toward their van.

"What are we going to do?"

"Take them down before Heather makes her next round."

When the first deader reached the van, Lisa stood and fired a single round into the top of its skull. The head erupted like a crushed pumpkin.

DAPHNE WAITED UNTIL the cart turned around the end of the vans, giving her a clear shot. On seeing Daphne inside the cage, Heather steered closer so she would have a better shot.

Daphne waited until the cart had passed before firing a round into the pack. The buckshot ripped apart the head of the nearest deader. It collapsed, leaving a smear of blood and gore across the cement. Several stray pellets tore into the deader on its left side, puncturing its face and gouging out its eye.

She fired five more shells into the pack, taking down three and ripping up two others.

Eleven of the living dead steered away and swarmed the

cage, their hands pulling on the chain links and their teeth trying to bite through the metal.

Daphne reloaded the Mossberg, praying the cage could withstand the pressure long enough for her to clear the pack.

HEATHER TURNED AT the conveyor belt, preparing to make a third run by the vans. She quickly glanced over her shoulder. The pack had been cut by almost two-thirds. This might work after all.

DORRIE HELD THE golf club above her head, waiting for the deader at the rear of the cart to climb close enough for her to strike it. The cart was half-filled with boxes and two rolled-up rugs, so the deader had to make its way across the pile to get to her. Every time the thing got near the top, Heather would take a corner, knocking it off balance. Then it would have to start the climb all over again. With each turn, the stack of boxes shifted and became unstable.

Which gave Dorrie an idea.

She wedged the golf club between the bars of the two carts, placing the clubhead behind the boxes. Seeing her so close, the deader became frantic and rushed up the pile. Dorrie checked in front of her. Heather was about to make the turn back toward the vans.

When the cart veered left, the pile of boxes tilted precariously. Dorrie jammed the club to her right. It moved the pile only a few inches, but enough to send them toppling over the side, taking the deader with them. It hit the floor and groaned as the heavy packages and two rugs fell on top of it.

"Yes."

Dorrie did not know if the boxes had killed the deader, but at least it would take a while for it to dig itself out.

AS PAUL WAS diverted onto the small conveyor, he saw the deader rip out Dawn's throat. Ed rushed over and tried to get it in a headlock, but Paul knew he could not hold on long.

Getting to his feet, which was difficult because of the belt's movement, Paul rushed down to the loading area. The deader pushed itself up, forcing both it and Ed into a standing position. Ed lost his footing and fell backward, falling against the frame of the bay and sliding down, stunned. Spinning around, the deader lunged.

Paul reached the end of the belt at the same time as the deader. He kicked his right leg, slamming his heel into the side of its head. The thing's head twisted to the right at a ninety-degree angle, accompanied by a loud snap. It collapsed in front of the conveyor.

The maneuver knocked Paul off balance. He fell back onto the belt, which carried him to the end. Paul rolled off, landing on the chest of the deader he had just incapacitated. Its abdomen burst open, showering Paul in gore and congealed blood. He stood up quickly and stepped away a few paces. Its milky eyes focused on him, its teeth snapping, but it could not—

A snarl caught Paul's attention. Shit, he had forgotten about the deader on the belt. It was only a few yards from the end.

Paul stepped back without looking behind him. There was no dock board between the bay and the rear of the truck, leaving a four-inch gap. His left leg fell through, becoming wedged at mid-thigh. Pain shot through his body. Paul twisted the leg, grateful it wasn't broken. He tried to extract it, but it was lodged in such a way he could not get enough leverage to free himself.

The deader rolled off the belt and landed on the first one. Paul heard the crack of a bone but was not certain which one suffered the break. The deader chasing him crawled to its feet and instantly collapsed, its left leg twisted at an ungodly angle.

Unable to walk, it pulled itself across the floor toward him.

Paul grabbed a large box of paper towels beside him and pushed it between himself and the deader. The thing banged into it, groaned, then started to crawl over the top. Paul used one hand to hold the box in place and the other to try and free his leg.

"Cover your eyes."

Ed had regained consciousness and stood behind the deader, holding a heavy package above his head. Paul turned his head as Ed brought the box down on the back of the deader's skull. The force pushed it into the box of paper towels, cushioning the blow. The back of its head had a long gash in it, but the thing still pulled itself up and went after Paul. Ed brought the box down again. This time, there was nothing to soften the strike. Its skull erupted, splattering Paul in even more human detritus.

Ed dropped the box and came around to help Paul.

"Thanks for saving me," said Ed.

"I could say the same thing."

When freed, Paul walked up and down the trailer. He limped, and the muscles hurt like hell, but nothing seemed broken or fractured.

"Okay," said Paul. "Let's go help the others."

"Neither of us are in shape to fight. Besides, at least half a dozen deaders are in the trailers down the line."

"I'll get my shotgun. It's by the conveyor."

"How many rounds do you have for it?"

"None," replied Paul, admitting defeat.

"Sorry, but we have to sit out the battle this time."

Ed reached up and closed the sliding door to the trailer.

AS HEATHER MADE the third trip around the facility, Lisa was ready. Heather drove close, giving Lisa a better shot. She took down four and wounded two more. Six more broke off and rushed her and Tumulty on top of the delivery van.

"This is easy," said Tumulty.

"Don't jinx us." She reloaded the Magnum and began taking out those beneath them.

Only five deaders still followed Heather and Dorrie.

HAZI NOTICED THE pile of bodies in front of the cage, trapping Daphne inside. When the cart made its second pass, she raced across the building to the cage.

Daphne appeared shocked. "What are you doing here?"

Hazi grabbed a deader from the top of the pile by the leg and pulled it to one side. "Clearing the cage for you."

"You know they're coming back for a third run?"

"I figured that, but I hated seeing you trapped here."

Daphne started to protest but thought otherwise. She could use all the help she could get.

As Hazi removed the bodies from in front of the cage, Daphne reloaded.

A few minutes later, gunfire broke out from the other side of the van.

"Get inside."

Hazi moved the last deader out of the way and joined Daphne.

When the cart came around, only five deaders followed. She waited until Heather passed by before firing six rounds in succession, taking down the last of the living dead.

"Is that it?" asked Hazi, a tone of uncertainty in her voice.

"For this side. Come on."

The two women exited the cage. As they did, Lisa and Tumulty joined them.

"Are you okay?" asked Lisa.

Daphne nodded, then reloaded her Mossberg.

With no more deaders pursuing them, Heather steered the cart into a U-turn and brought it back, stopping in front of

Daphne.

"You get the last of them?"

"In this area."

"What can I say?" Heather smiled. "DeadEx, when it absolutely, positively, has to be killed overnight."

Hazi groaned at the pun.

Lisa shook her head. "Sounds like something Paul would say."

Shit, Paul. During all the excitement, she had forgotten he was on the other side of the building. She hoped nothing had happened to him.

"We need to check on the others and clear out any deaders still inside." She opened three boxes of shotgun shells and piled them in her pockets. "Who here knows how to use a gun?"

Heather and Hazi raised their hands.

"What about you?" she asked Tumulty.

"My grandfather took me shooting when I was ten, but that was twenty years ago."

"You'll learn quickly. Follow me."

"Where?"

"To get you all armed up."

Daphne led the way to the van in Slot Twenty-Six, where boxes with weapons had been stacked. She opened the top box, removed a Savage Stevens 320 pump-action shotgun, and focused on Hazi.

"Can you handle one of these?"

"You bet." Hazi took the shotgun.

Daphne pointed to the van's interior. "There are 12-gauge rounds in there. Load up with as many as you can carry."

Heather got a Browning AB3 bolt-action hunting rifle, and Tumulty a Ruger bolt-action rifle. Once everyone had loaded their weapons and stocked up on ammunition, Daphne led them into the other section of the facility.

WITH THE TRUCK engines shut down and the deaders in the parking lot taken care of, those outside the facility could hear the gunfire inside.

Donnelly looked at the others. "Should we go in and help them?"

"With what?" asked Johnny. "We don't have any weapons."

"We just can't leave them there," protested Joey.

"I don't want to get eaten—"

"It's easy," interrupted Polozov. "You three get in trailer and back it up to dock. If there's trouble, we pull away and crush them in parking lot again. Sound good?"

The others agreed and climbed into the trailer. When they were ready, Polozov restarted the truck, maneuvered the trailer toward the building, and slowly backed into the bay.

DAPHNE'S GROUP CLEARED out the small vehicle loading area first, finding Daniel and Annabelle. After arming the couple, they made their way down to the unloading dock, where they found the trailer that held the deaders as well as the devoured remnants of Ian. From there, they continued along the conveyor belt toward the loading bays.

The sound of the living dead feasting could be heard as they approached Bay Four. Daphne held up her hand for everyone to stop and motioned for them to raise their weapons. When ready, Daphne banged the stock of the Mossberg several times against the steel frame of the conveyor.

Snarling came from inside the trailer, followed by four deaders racing out the back, covered in fresh blood and pieces of flesh. A barrage of gunfire brought them down in seconds. An eerie silence fell over the facility.

"Paul, are you here?" Daphne's voice quivered, fearful when he did not respond.

Continuing down the line, the sound of a truck backing up

echoed through the open door of Bay Nine. A few seconds later, Johnny, Joey, and Donnelly stepped out. The sight of Daphne and the others startled Donnelly until he realized they were not the living dead.

"What's going on in here?" he asked.

Lisa lowered her Magnum. "A horde of deaders got loose."

"We know," said Johnny. "We saw them take down Medugno."

Donnelly looked around. "Any losses in here?"

"Too many," answered Heather.

"Is Paul with you?" Daphne asked anxiously.

Donnelley shook his head. "We haven't seen him since those things attacked."

Tears filled Daphne's eyes, and she fought back the urge to break down. Lisa placed her hand around the woman's shoulder and hugged her.

Hazi pointed to the closed door of Bay Eight, the body of Dawn lying off to the side. "We haven't checked in there."

"What's the use?" sniffed Daphne.

"Let's try." Lisa escorted her friend down to the bay.

Those with weapons spread out, ready to fire. Lisa looked over to Donnelly and motioned toward the door. The driver stepped over, pulled up the door, and jumped to one side.

Ed and Paul were inside, Ed standing a few feet from the door holding a heavy package over his head, and Paul holding the two-wheel hand cart in his hands, ready to shove the nose plate into a deader's face. Both men lowered their makeshift weapons and sighed with relief. Paul dropped down on a large box and rubbed his left leg.

Daphne rushed into the trailer and threw her arms around Paul, embracing him so tightly she almost knocked him over.

"I thought you were…." She stifled back tears.

Paul hugged her back. "It's going to take more than a few deaders to take me down."

"A few?" Heather asked, astounded. "There had to be

almost a hundred of those things."

"They hit us pretty bad," added Lisa.

The realization hit Paul hard. "How many?"

Daphne grimaced. "Five, including Ian."

"Damn." Paul sighed and ran his palm over his scalp. His attitude switched from relieved back to serious. He stood, stumbling slightly when he put pressure on his left leg.

Daphne grew concerned. "Were you bit?"

"I caught it between the truck and the loading dock." Paul thought for a moment, then turned to Polozov. "Are the trucks ready?"

"We just need to load them."

"Good. Let's load up and get out of here."

"What about the stuff we haven't gone through yet?" asked Tumulty.

"Give it a quick sort through. Bring everything you found down here."

"We can use the cart for that," said Heather. "It'll make it easier."

"Let's get to it. I want to be on the road in an hour."

Chapter Four

I T TOOK JUST under three hours to sort through the rest of the facility, bring everything of value down to the bays, and load them aboard the trucks. The extra two hours proved to be worth it. When finished, the group had scavenged eighteen semi-automatic weapons and rifles; enough ammo to hold off a small army of the living dead; outdoor footwear and clothes to outfit everyone at camp; two cots, three sleeping bags, a tent, plus almost two dozen blankets; and tires, oil, and sundry automotive supplies. Unfortunately, they were not as successful in finding other essentials. The team discovered seven cases of canned beans and soup, plus thirteen boxes of various junk food. Even worse, they found only six cases of bottled water, barely enough to last a few days. As for medications, other than the ten shots of Insulin for Ed, all they could dig up were a few prescriptions of little value, several over-the-counter medications, and quite a few bottles of vitamins and supplements.

Everyone agreed that leaving behind their fallen comrades would be disrespectful. Once the supplies had been loaded, their bodies, or in some cases what little remained of them, were placed at the rear of one of the trailers to have a proper burial at camp.

The trip back to the compound was uneventful. The convoy arrived at the compound late in the afternoon. Those who stayed behind rushed out to greet them. Paul, Daphne, Polozov, and Donnelly met Torosian as he approached.

"Thank God, you made it back. We were getting worried."

"We ran into horde of *zhivye mertvetsy* inside," said Polozov.

"*Zhivye mertvetsy?*" asked Daphne.

"Russian for living dead."

Torosian looked at the rest of the team heading for the trailer, noticing some were missing. "How many?"

"Five," answered Paul. "Dawn, Dunnan, French, Medugno, and one of my own."

Torosian lowered his head and said a silent prayer.

"We brought the remains back to give them a proper burial."

Torosian raised his head. "Thank you. We can do that before dinner. Was the haul worth it?"

"In some respects, yes."

Paul headed for the rear of Polozov's trailer, motioning for Torosian to follow. Donnelly went ahead and unsecured the latch. As the others joined him, he lifted the sliding door, revealing everything stacked inside. Donnelly whistled.

"Impressive."

"Thanks. We retrieved bedding and clothes for everyone here, plus enough firearms and ammo to keep the compound safe from anything that comes after you."

Torosian seemed confused. "You mean deaders."

"Or humans. With society collapsing, so does law and social order."

"We packed the weapons and clothes near the end so they'll be easy to get to," added Donnelly.

"Good. What about food and water?"

"We weren't as fortunate there. We only found six cases of bottled water and food to last three days, a week if you ration it. And most of it is junk food. Medicines were in short supply. A lot of vitamins and over-the-counter stuff, but nothing that'll help with infections or anything like that. Oh, does anyone here have diabetes?"

Torosian shrugged. "Not that I know of, but I can ask around. Why?"

"We found a box of insulin. Ed is diabetic and about to run out of his meds. If anyone here needs some, we can divvy it up."

"I appreciate that." Torosian glanced at his watch and then back into the trailer. "Let's get the weapons and clothes unloaded. We've all been wearing the same stuff for several days and can use a change." For the first time, he noticed those who had gone on the supply run were covered in blood and gore. "You all need to get out of those clothes and burn them before you stink up the compound and attract every wild animal within a five-mile radius."

"What about unloading the trucks?" asked Daphne.

"I have enough able-bodied people here to do that. Every one of you, go clean yourselves up. I'll have some new clothes sent over to you soon."

ONCE THOSE WHO went on the supply run had cleaned up and the weapons had been distributed, Torosian held a memorial service for those who had not survived. Volunteers from the lumbering crew had dug the graves and buried the bodies earlier, digging five separate plots rather than the indignity of a mass grave. Torosian said a few words about how brave the fallen were, especially Dunnan and Dawn, who gave their lives to save others. Paul could not help but notice that the plots for Ian, Medugno, and French were much smaller than those for the other two.

Afterward, the group ate dinner around the campfire. Several who did not go kept asking about what had happened at the facility, but the team did not want to relive the nightmare. A few of the more insensitive ones kept nagging, and Paul could tell Daphne was about ready to light into them, so he changed the subject.

"What are you going to do with the truck and trailers?

Dump them somewhere?"

"Hell, no. We got plans for them." Torosian pointed over his shoulder to where the trailer that had carried back the bodies sat. "We're going to weld steel plates to both sides of one trailer and use it to block the road leading up here. It'll be a lot easier than trying to build a roadblock, and we can move it when we need to get in or out. The other one we'll use as housing so everyone isn't living in that small trailer."

"Good. Nothing goes to waste." Paul paused for a moment. "Which reminds me, what are the chances of commandeering one of the vehicles down there on the road? I have seven people and a dog stuffed into one Honda Pilot. I sure could use another set of wheels."

"I got you covered on that. There's a company pick-up behind the trailer. You can have that. It's the least I can do."

"Won't you get into trouble with corporate?" asked Lisa.

Torosian chuckled. "Everyone at corporate is mindlessly stumbling around the office like they usually do. Don't worry about it."

"I appreciate it."

Torosian became serious. "By the way, I asked around, and no one here has diabetes, so the insulin is yours. How did you want to divvy up the rest of the stuff?"

"We'll be on the road, so we'll have a better chance of re-supplying than you. I was thinking one case of bottled water and one case of baked beans."

Torosian nodded. "Sounds reasonable."

Daphne chimed in. "If you have enough, another change of clothes for each of us. We have a habit of getting dirty."

"Dirty?" Hazi laughed out loud. "We all came back from FedEx looking like the deaders."

Daniel and Annabelle fidgeted in their seats and focused on the ground.

"What's wrong?" asked Lisa.

Annabelle glanced up. Her voice wavered. "We're wearing

the same clothes we did when we left because we didn't get involved in the fight."

"So?" asked Daphne.

"So?" snapped Daniel, his anger directed at himself. "Every one of you fought the deaders while we stayed safely hidden. We were useless."

Paul leaned forward and made eye contact with Daniel. "And if you had tried to do anything, there would be seven graves over there rather than five. You had no weapons and nothing to defend yourself with. What could you have done?"

"Dunnan grabbed a kayak and held back those things so Tumulty could get to safety. What did I do?"

"You protected the most valuable person to you," said Daphne with a soft, reassuring tone. "You saved your wife."

The anger faded, replaced by self-recrimination. "I could have saved her and tried to help."

"You would have saved her then been eaten alive," Paul reassured him. "For nothing. You'd be dead, and Annabelle would be left alone to fend for herself in this shithole of a world. What would have happened to her then?"

Daniel sniffed back tears of shame. "I could have done something."

"You did." Annabelle took his left hand and raised it to her lips, tenderly kissing the knuckles. "Don't you remember? Those things almost broke into the van, and it took the two of us to stop them. If you hadn't joined me, I'd be dead, too."

Daniel started to speak but stopped, not knowing what to say.

"You can't save the world," added Ed. "You can only try and save the ones you love. We've been fighting the living dead since day one. I lost my wife two days ago and will never get over it."

"I watched my father die and then attack us," said Toshii.

"I killed my mother to prevent her from becoming one of those things," added Lisa.

Daniel looked at each of them and swallowed hard. "I'm sorry. I shouldn't be whining."

"You're not whining." Polozov, who sat to Daniel's right, wrapped his hand around Daniel's shoulder. "You're adjusting to apocalypse. We all are."

"Thanks." Daniel patted the Russian's hand.

Polozov switched to his usual upbeat self. "Besides, next time, you'll have weapon to defend Missus. Then you can kick deader ass."

"Which brings up another point," Torosian said cautiously. "How are we going to divvy up the weapons?"

Paul thought for a second. "I was thinking we'd take the three AK-47s so everyone in our group will be armed. The rounds we found for them won't work on any other gun. Since you don't have any handguns, we'll take the .40 caliber for the Glock and the .357 rounds for the Magnum."

"What about the shotgun rounds?"

"How about a thirty-seventy split, with you getting the bigger portion?"

"Sounds fair to me." Torosian turned to the others. "Anyone disagree?"

Not surprisingly, the only one who did was Pam. "Why are they getting such a large share of our stuff? We outnumber them four to one. We need as many guns as we can get. Besides, they got four of our people killed."

Donnelly sighed. "For Christ's sake Pam, shut the fuck up."

She became defiant. "I will not."

Gojira growled at the woman, but Toshii held the dog in place.

"Yesterday you bitched about bringing any weapons onto the compound. Now you want to keep all the guns. Stop being a hypocrite."

"I take offense at that." Pam crossed her arms across her chest.

"Don't," snapped Torosian. "You wouldn't have the clothes you're wearing or the food you'll be eating if it wasn't for these people. Listen to Donnelly and shut the fuck up."

"I have a right to speak—"

"No, you don't." Torosian shifted to glare at Pam. "I got news for you. All those precious rights you're spouting about died along with the rest of society. There's no more Constitution. No more courts. No more politics. Until we get things back in order, it's survival of the fittest."

"I never," huffed Pam.

"And it shows," laughed Polozov.

Pam ignored the Russian. "I think we should take a vote on this."

"Knock it off." Torosian yelled at her so vehemently it caught everyone off guard. "This is not a democracy anymore. I took you and the others into this compound, and my crew has been protecting you. I'm in charge. Shit, you're so lazy you didn't even help unload the trailers. If you don't like how I do things, you're welcome to leave. That goes for the rest of you. Any takers?"

Everyone shook their heads. A couple of people gave Torosian the thumbs up.

"Do you have anything else to say?" The way Torosian spoke made it clear it was more of an order to shut up than a question.

Pam bowed her head and said nothing.

The foreman turned back to Paul, his demeanor once again pleasant. "Take whatever you need."

"Thank you."

"I'll give you twice the water and ammo if you take Pam with you."

She looked up, shock and fear in her eyes.

"What the hell would we use her for?" asked Daphne.

"Bait?" Akiko smiled.

Several members of Torosian's group laughed, causing Pam to storm off in a huff.

"When are you leaving?" asked Torosian. "You're welcome to stay here if you want. We could use your help."

"Thanks, but we're trying to make it to either the Midwest or the northern states. We have a better chance of surviving the fewer people there are around us."

"How do you plan to get there?" asked Donnelly.

"The Appalachian Trail. It's not far from here. It'll take us down to Georgia just north of Atlanta. I figure there won't be many people on it."

"I got better idea," interrupted Polozov. "Appalachian Trail is only for hiking. You'll have to carry all your stuff by hand. And if you're attacked by *zhivye mertvetsy*, you have nowhere to run. Even if you make it to end, you'll be in heavily populated area of Georgia. Try Skyline Drive. It's auto trail that runs through mountains. Very beautiful. I've done it before. Reminds me of Urals. It comes out near West Virginia and Tennessee. Probably little traffic on it, so you'll have less chance of running into trouble. And, once you make it off Skyline Drive, you still have your vehicles."

"That does sound like a better idea." Paul turned to the others. "What do you think?"

Daphne nodded. "It makes more sense."

"We get to keep the vehicles," added Ed. "Which means we can travel farther and faster."

"It'll be safer for the kids," said Akiko.

Lisa agreed.

Paul turned back to Torosian. "How do we get there?"

"It's not too far," said Torosian. "About... what, forty miles?"

"Closer to sixty," corrected the Russian. "Don't worry. We have map in office. I'll make copy for you, and we can go over route later."

"Thanks."

"Then it's settled." Torosian slapped his knees and stood. "Polozov will make sure you know how to get there. If you need anything else, let me know and it's yours. If I were you, I'd get some rest. You're going to have a few rough days ahead of you."

Chapter Five

D APHNE LEANED HER Mossberg against the passenger seat of the Pilot and placed her bag of shotgun shells on the floor. She was not thrilled about hitting the road again, especially considering what they had gone through since leaving Pittsburgh. But it was better than staying at the logging camp. Assuming that Torosian could fortify the camp, and taking into consideration their new-found weapons, this location remained close to too many highly populated areas. While safe for now, if any masses of the living dead began wandering and stumbled across the compound, Torosian's people did not stand a chance. And that horde they encountered in Leesburg probably still followed them. Right now, the safest place is on the road.

Besides, there were too many people here with too many differing viewpoints. If the deaders did not disrupt things here, internal strife would.

She closed the door to the Pilot and looked around. Akiko watched Toshii and Judith play with Gojira, all of them waiting for the word to load up to get underway. Ed and Lisa finished packing their supplies, half in the Pilot and half in the Dodge RAM Torosian had given them, ensuring that if one vehicle was lost or abandoned, they would still have food and water. One member of the group was missing.

"Where's Paul?"

Judith pointed to where they had buried the others last night. "He said he wanted to put on his specs before we left."

"She means pay his respect," whispered Akiko.

Daphne snickered, then headed out to find Paul.

As Judith said, Daphne found him standing in front of the three freshly dug graves. He put his weight on his right leg, favoring the bruised left. She wrapped her arms around his and leaned her head on his shoulder.

"Are you ready to hit the road?"

Paul did not answer, instead focusing his gaze on the mounds of dirt. His expression was a mixture of depression and self-loathing.

"What's wrong?" When Paul did not respond, she squeezed his arm between hers. "Come on, hon. Talk to me."

"I shouldn't be leading this group anymore."

The statement caught her off guard. "Do you mean you no longer want to lead it?"

"No. I mean, I don't deserve to be leading this group."

"Why would you think that?"

Paul gently broke her grip on his arm. "Five people are dead because of me."

"Five people are dead because a horde of deaders got loose inside the facility. They did the killing, not you."

"Well...." Paul hesitated. "I might as well have killed them. I hid in the trailer where it was safe while you and Lisa cleaned out the deaders."

That's what this is all about, thought Daphne. "That's your ego talking."

Paul bristled. At first, Daphne thought he would chew her out but, after a few seconds, his demeanor shifted back to putting himself down. He turned to walk away. Daphne moved in front of him, forcing him to stop.

"No one else is more qualified to lead our group than you. You rescued me, Akiko, Toshii, and Lisa. We all would have died on that bridge if you hadn't figured out how to get us across. And I know Lisa would stand by you after saving Judith. No one else could have gotten us this far."

"You don't understand." Paul turned, took a few steps, then faced Daphne. "You found me hiding inside the trailer like… like a coward. I should have been out there fighting those things like the rest of you."

"You drew off some of the deaders to give Ed and Dawn a chance, then wound up getting stuck on the overhead conveyor belt."

Paul's mouth dropped open slightly. "Ed told me. He also told me that you saved his life. What more do you want?"

"Damn it. You found me holed up inside the trailer."

"What else were you supposed to do? You could barely walk, ran out of ammo, and had nothing to use as a weapon."

Paul turned away, ashamed of himself.

"So, what you told Daniel was a lie?" she asked.

Paul spun around to face her. "Not at all."

"You told him it was okay for them to lock himself in the van because he had no way to fight the deaders and would have gotten eaten for nothing. What's the difference between what he did and what you and Ed did?"

Paul's shoulders slumped. "I should have been out there battling those things."

"And you would have died for no good reason," Daphne snapped at him. She moved closer, taking his cheeks gently in her hands, her tome mellowing. "Sure, Ed or I could take over, but we wouldn't survive a week. You're the only one who can get us through this because you have the skills, the knowledge, and the balls. Believe me, I can attest to the latter."

Paul broke into a smile.

"That's the Paul I know. You have to keep yourself safe so you can lead the rest of us to safety. Besides, I kinda like you." Daphne leaned forward and kissed him tenderly. "Let's get back. The others are worried about you. And we have to hit the road."

Taking Paul's hand in hers, Daphne led him back to their vehicles, walking slowly to accommodate his limp.

Torosian and Polozov were waiting for them by the Pilot.

"Come to say goodbye?" asked Paul.

"That, and to give you the map to get you to Front Royal."

Polozov spread several sheets of 8x11 paper on the hood showing maps of the area. Arrows drawn in ink ran along various roads. "I've plotted out safest route to get to Skyline Drive. These avoid major population centers. Problem is you have to go through Front Royal to get to auto trail. It's more than likely overrun by the *zhivye mertvetsy*. Good news is, you only have to go through outskirts of city to get there, so with luck, you'll be okay. Any questions?"

Daphne glanced over the maps since she would be the navigator. "Looks clear cut to me."

"*Spasibo*." Polozov shook Paul's hand and hugged Daphne. "Good luck to all of you."

Torosian stepped forward. "I don't suppose there's anything I can say to get you to stay."

"We have our own plans," said Paul. "No offense."

"None taken." The foreman offered his hand to Paul and Daphne. "Thanks again for everything."

"Our pleasure. I hope we run into you again when this is over." Paul turned to the others. "Mount up. We're heading out."

Everyone climbed into their respective vehicles, and Paul led the mini convoy down the access road. Daphne checked her side mirror. Torosian and Polozov waved goodbye.

Chapter Six

PAUL TURNED RIGHT off the access road onto Route 7, passed the sign warning about deaders ahead, and drove west. Akiko, Toshii, and Gojira sat in back. Ed followed in the RAM with Lisa and Judith.

"I hope we're not staying on this road," said Paul. "This looks like it'll take us through every town in the area."

"It will, so we'll be getting off it soon. In fact…" Daphne pointed ahead of them. "…turn left onto 704."

They entered a two-lane back road lined with trees.

Daphne checked the map. "Keep on this road then, in a few miles, turn right onto 725. It adds several miles to the trip but avoids all the towns in the area."

Other than a single abandoned SUV with a flat tire and a lone deader with a leg devoured to the bone stumbling along the shoulder, they encountered no incidents. After fifteen minutes, they came to the end of the road.

"Turn right here. You'll hit a hairpin turn that'll put you back on Route 7, then make an immediate left onto 601."

"Thank God you know how to read a map," joked Paul.

"I'll admit, GPS is easier."

A few minutes later, they were on 601 heading south.

"If Polozov is right, we follow a few secondary roads for a little over forty miles before we reach Front Royal."

Akiko leaned between the two seats. "How large is Front Royal?"

"The map says it's good-sized, but nothing like Washington

or Leesburg."

"What about those things?" asked Akiko. "Are we going to have to fight our way through them?"

"We might have to," Paul answered.

"I don't think so." Daphne held up the maps. "Polozov took care of that."

A LITTLE MORE than half an hour into the trip, they still had not encountered anything other than wildlife and a flock of wild turkeys crossing the road, which blocked their path for a few minutes. The only sign of the apocalypse came from a pillar of black smoke rising from the horizon.

Daphne constantly referred to the map, checking it with the streets they passed to make certain they remained on the correct route. A green sign stood on the shoulder ahead of them.

Front Royal   5 miles

"Pull over here," she ordered.

Paul looked around for danger, not spotting anything. "Is something wrong?"

Daphne pointed to the sign. "We're almost there. Pull over so I can confer with Ed."

Paul slowed to a stop, lowered the window, and waved for Ed to pull up beside him. Ed obliged. As he pulled to a stop beside the Pilot, Lisa rolled down the passenger window.

"What's up?"

"We're near Front Royal. I wanted to pass along Polozov's directions in case we get separated."

"Good idea," said Ed.

"Do you have a piece of paper?"

Lisa opened the glove compartment and rummaged

through it, eventually pulling out a small notebook and a pen.

"Go ahead."

Daphne read aloud the directions the Russian had provided while Lisa diligently jotted them down. When finished, Daphne asked, "Do they make sense?"

Lisa nodded.

"One more thing," she added. "I-66 is up ahead. If it's like every other major highway we've passed, it's more than likely gridlocked with traffic and swarming with deaders. There are no ramps to the highway, but the chances are good that some of the deaders, maybe quite a few, have wandered up the overpass and are all over this road, so be careful."

"What if we can't get through?" asked Ed.

"We have to. It's the only way to reach Skyline Drive."

"Let's assume worst-case scenario," said Lisa.

Paule leaned to the side in front of Daphne. "If we can't get through, fall back to this location, and we'll go from there."

"Roger that."

Daphne waved. "Good luck."

"You, too," replied Lisa.

Paul accelerated and headed for Front Royal. Daphne made sure the Mossberg was loaded and opened the duffel bag in case she needed more ammo. In the back, Akiko reached over Gojira and hugged Toshii's left hand. The kid squeezed back but kept his revolver in his right hand in case he needed it. Sensing the increased tension in the SUV, Gojira sat up in his seat, his ears folded back on his head.

They soon arrived at the I-66 overpass. Paul concentrated on the pack of more than thirty deaders spread across the road.

"Will we make it through?" asked Daphne.

"Not a problem."

She chuckled. "You're a terrible liar."

On hearing the approaching vehicles, the deaders looked around for the source of the noise. One deader in a tattered and blood-soaked State Police uniform spotted them, snarled, and charged. The others fell in line behind it.

Paul maneuvered as far right as possible, the tires only inches from the shoulder, and pushed his foot down on the accelerator. The distance closed rapidly. Paul switched on his left directional, warning Ed of his intentions.

When twenty feet from the pack, Paul swerved into the left lane and raced past. Ed followed a few feet to his rear. The sudden switch caught the deaders off guard. They turned to attack the two vehicles, but Paul had made it through by then. He checked his rearview mirror. Ed was still a few yards behind, but the deaders chased the two vehicles.

Ahead of them sat Front Royal and, just beyond the town, the peaks of the Blue Ridge Mountains. The source of the smoke they had spotted earlier was a conflagration on the northern outskirts of town that, judging by the size, consumed several blocks. A hundred yards ahead, the police had set up a roadblock on the main road. Half a dozen vehicles were parked on either shoulder, leaving two police cars and a pair of wooden horses blocking the path. The way beyond was clear except for several hundred deaders roaming through town. On hearing the sound of engines, they looked around until one of the living dead at the rear of the pack spotted the approaching vehicles. The deader snarled and broke into a run, with the others falling in behind it. Paul had no idea how they would get out of this.

"Slow down," warned Daphne. She pointed to a small road a few yards ahead on the left. "That's our turn."

Paul spun the steering wheel to the left. The tires screeched as the Pilot swung into the curve, the backend fishtailing. For a moment, he thought they might flip over or swerve off the road, either of which would be a death sentence with the attacking swarm. Luckily, the SUV righted itself at the last minute and roared ahead. Paul checked his mirror. His maneuver had warned Ed about the turn, giving the latter enough time to make it without overturning.

"Next time, warn me when we're about to make a turn."

Daphne extended the middle finger of her left hand as she studied the map clutched in her right. "You navigate and I'll drive."

Paul gritted his teeth but did not respond.

"This road ends in less than a mile. When it does, turn right."

"WHAT THE FUCK!" Ed applied the brakes, slowing down the RAM enough to make the turn. "He must be trying to avoid those deaders ahead."

"According to Daphne's directions, that's the turn we needed to take." Then Ed's statement dawned on her. "What deaders?"

Ed used his head to motion toward Front Royal. She looked up, shocked at the sight of so many living dead chasing after them.

"This is as bad as Leesburg."

"It's like this everywhere," Ed replied. "The world is dead, and we're unfortunate enough to have survived."

Lisa turned to respond but stopped. The road they were on paralleled I-66 to their left. She was not prepared for the nightmarish scene.

The highway was gridlocked with vehicles, creating an expanse of chaos. The doors to every vehicle were open, the occupants having tried to escape the living dead. Lisa doubted any did. Hundreds of deaders sauntered between the lines of vehicles. She could not even imagine the horror as those trapped inside their cars watched as a tidal wave of the living dead washed down the highway, consuming everything in its path. Her gaze focused on a Mercedes sitting on the shoulder, its passenger door opened, and what used to be a young woman belted into the passenger seat. The flesh and muscles on its right arm and chest had been eaten away. It thrashed its head from side to side, trapped in the car for eternity.

On hearing the vehicles drive by, several deaders turned, flowed down the embankment, and ran after them. Within seconds, a few hundred living dead rushed after them.

From the back, Judith cried. "Mommy, I'm scared."

Lisa shifted in her seat, reached back with her left hand, and clasped her daughter's wrist.

"It'll be okay, honey. We've been through worse."

She only hoped that her last words to her daughter were not a lie.

PAUL SLOWED AS he neared the end of the road, getting ready to make the turn.

In the back deck, Gojira started barking. Toshii reached over to comfort the dog.

"What's wrong with him?" asked Akiko.

"That." Toshii motioned out the left rear window.

Akiko turned to see what her son referred to and gasped. Like dominoes falling one after the other, every deader on I-66 rushed down the embankment heading for them. She leaned forward and tapped Paul on the shoulder.

"You might want to speed up."

"Why do you—" Paul glanced over at his side mirror. "Fuck."

"What are you—" Daphne turned and saw the approaching swarm. She checked her map. "When you make the turn, you have about two miles before you reach town, so floor it."

"You don't have to tell me twice. Akiko, Toshii, let me know if they start to get too close."

Trees stood off to the right, blocking his view of the upcoming road. Paul slowed just enough to make the turn without losing control. The road ahead was lined on both sides with forest, and nothing lay ahead. He waited until Ed also made the turn, then pushed his foot down on the gas pedal until the

Pilot reached a speed of eighty-two miles per hour.

"What now?"

"This will bring us right to Route 340. Take a left there, and the entrance to Skyline Drive will be on your left."

Residential homes appeared on either side of the road, a few at first, but increasing in number the closer they got to the center of town.

"We're almost there," said Paul. "Everyone, keep your eyes open for trouble."

Thankfully, the only deaders were a handful stumbling along the side streets leading into the local neighborhoods. If he hit one at this speed, that would be it for the four of them.

Commercial buildings came into view ahead. Paul lifted his foot off the accelerator. As the SUV slowed, he checked his rearview mirror. They had left the horde of deaders far behind, although he knew they were pursuing them and would eventually catch up unless he hauled ass.

"Watch out!" yelled Daphne.

Paul switched his attention to the front. A few hundred feet ahead, the intersection they had to pass through was blocked by a multi-vehicle accident. He quickly assessed the situation. There was no way to maneuver through it and, even if there was, scores of the living dead sauntered around the accident scene. Their attention was drawn to the approaching vehicles. One of them spotted the Pilot, snarled, and raced toward it, with the rest falling in behind.

With only seconds to act, Paul turned right, bouncing over the curb and racing into the parking lot of a commercial complex. The pack gave chase.

ED SAW THE approaching danger and prepared to follow Paul. However, the deaders racing after the Pilot blocked his path, making it impossible to keep up. He turned left, skidding into a Kentucky Fried Chicken parking lot.

Still comforting her daughter, Lisa slammed her chest against the side of the driver's seat. She turned around in time to see them racing through the parking lot.

"You lost Paul." Her tone dripped with fear.

"There's no way I could have kept up with them with all those things—"

A naked deader, the upper half of its body torn to shreds, stepped in front of the RAM. Ed swerved to the right to go around it. The left front fender caught the thing in the chest. It ricocheted off the pick-up, flew across the parking lot, and slammed into the side of the fast-food restaurant, splattering against the wall. Ed exited at the end of the lot and swerved left onto the road, fishtailing the RAM. He was now heading in the opposite direction of Paul with nearly seventy deaders chasing him.

"Mommy, I'm scared."

Lisa started to turn around to comfort her daughter. Ed grabbed the woman's arm and forced her to face forward.

"No time for that. I need you to help me find a way to Route 340 or we're screwed."

AKIKO CRIED OUT as she was thrown against the door by the sudden turn.

"Are you okay?" asked Paul.

"Yes. Just warn me next time, please."

"I will if I have—"

"Off to your left," called out Daphne.

A female deader raced around the corner of the CVS and rushed them. Paul did not have time to avoid it, hitting it with the left fender. Its abdomen ruptured as the body bounced off the hood, slid up the windshield, and rolled off to the side, leaving a streak of congealed blood and gore along the glass. Paul leaned to one side so he could see past the smear.

The end of the parking lot rapidly approached. Paul

checked his rearview mirror. The horde of deaders was closing fast. He slowed down just enough to maneuver toward the exit and swung right onto South Commerce Avenue. The two lanes ahead leading into the intersection were clogged with traffic. Luckily for them, the right lanes were open, but they led into the center of town.

"Where do I go?"

"Calm down." Daphne consulted the map. "There's a road up ahead on the left. That'll take us back to 340."

Paul's gaze alternated between what was ahead of him and searching for the road. He spotted it after a few seconds.

"Shit!"

Daphne lifted her head from the map. "What now?"

"The traffic's blocking it. I can't make the turn."

"There's another turn a few hundred feet ahead."

Paul sped up, putting as much distance as possible between himself and the pursuing horde of deaders. A few seconds later, he spotted the road on the left.

"That one's also blocked."

"Just keep going until you find one that's open."

Easier said than done. Another jam prevented him from turning down the third street.

"If we keep this up, we'll be in the downtown area in a few—"

"There!" Daphne pointed left.

An intersection sat directly ahead, all the lanes clear except for a few abandoned vehicles.

Paul slowed to weave his way through. As he made the turn, he leaned his head toward the back seat.

"How are we doing?"

Akiko looked out the rear window. The horde had grown even larger as more deaders joined from the side streets. Because Paul had to slow down to make the turn, they were catching up.

"They're getting closer. About two hundred feet away."

"Damn."

The road was an entrance into another commercial complex. Paul had planned on turning left. However, on seeing the Pilot make the turn, the swarm did the same and poured into the parking lot. Heading in that direction would be suicide. Instead, he swung the steering wheel to the right, going around the stores.

"Talk to me."

Daphne waved him off, concentrating on the map. She glanced up, frustration and fear in her expression, then broke into a smile.

"That's the twin center off to the left. Turn left at the end of this road."

Paul reached the end, turned left, and slammed on the brakes. A fire truck blocked their path, the block of buildings behind it a smoldering pile of ashes and charred structural supports. He turned the steering wheel right and accelerated, racing down the road.

The swarm had closed to within one hundred feet.

Daphne frantically studied the maps, then slapped her hand against the paper. "Turn left the first chance you get."

Paul did, swerving the Pilot onto Crescent Street.

"I don't fucking believe this."

ED HEADED SOUTH as Lisa tried to figure out how to get back on course. When he checked his side mirrors, most of the deaders in the intersection had gone after Paul. Only a dozen or so followed them. Thank God for small favors.

But that also meant Paul and the others faced a greater chance of being overrun.

Another bit of luck. Since they were heading south out of Front Royal, there were only a small number of the living dead around.

"Where do we go from here?" he asked.

"I'd take your first right. Hopefully, that'll lead us to 340."

After driving for a minute, a road appeared to their right. Ed slowed and made the turn, then accelerated.

"Mommy, are we going to be okay?"

Lisa shifted in her seat, reached in the back, and held her daughter's hand. "Yes, honey. There's nothing to worry about."

"What about Toshii and the others?"

"They'll catch up with us."

"Promise?"

Lisa forced a smile. "I promise."

"We lucked out," said Ed.

Lisa turned around to face the front. "What do you mean?"

Ed pointed ahead of him. "There's Route 340."

He slowed as he approached the intersection, stopping at the end of the street. Other than the few deaders chasing them, there were no others around. Ed turned left onto 340 and headed south. A few seconds later, they came across signs with arrows pointing left directing them to Skyline Drive. Ed decreased speed as they drew near, then mumbled, "Shit."

A two-and-a-half-ton National Guard transport blocked access to Skyline Drive.

"I DON'T FUCKING believe this."

Paul had turned directly in front of the E. Wilson Morrison Elementary School. Two National Guard Humvees and an armored personnel carrier, as well as two school buses and a State Police car, were parked at the drop-off area. A wooden board ten feet square leaned up against one of the Humvees, the words EMERGENCY RELOCATION CENTER painted in red. Like every such center, somebody had snuck in after being bitten, turned, and infected the compound. Hundreds of deaders infested the area, most behind the improvised chain link fence surrounding the faculty parking lot. Close to thirty milled around in front of the school, their attention focusing on the Pilot as it approached.

Paul pushed his foot down on the accelerator. The Pilot raced past the school. Five deaders slammed into the right side of the SUV, leaving bloody streaks along the windows. The helmet of a National Guard deader struck the back window, fracturing the glass. Gojira growled and snapped at the thing, then continued barking as it bounced off the vehicle and rolled across the pavement.

Paul followed the street as it veered left.

"Daphne?"

"I'm on it." She studied the map. "Take the next right onto Main Street, then an immediate left. That'll put us on 340."

When he reached the intersection, Paul hesitated for a few seconds. The pack was seventy-five feet behind them. He pulled out into the intersection and turned left.

"No." Daphne pointed in the opposite direction. "I said right then left."

"I know. But those things are too close. If we lead them to 340, they'll follow us to Skyline Drive. We've got to lead them away first."

ED PARKED THE RAM in the center of the road beside the deuce-and-a-half, shifted into PARK, and left the engine running.

"Take over for me."

"What do you mean?" asked Lisa.

"I'm going to try and move the truck. If any deaders come after us, get out of here."

"I'm not going to leave you."

Ed motioned in the back toward Judith. "You can't let anything happen to her."

Lisa closed her eyes and nodded.

Grabbing his AK-47, Ed opened the door. He listened for

the sound of any approaching deaders and, not hearing any, climbed out.

Lisa opened her door. Before she could get out, Judith jumped forward between the seats and clutched her mother's arm, crying.

"Don't leave me."

"I'm not, hon. I'm changing places with Ed."

"You promise?"

"I promise." Lisa gently removed her daughter's hand. She got out, closed the door, circled around the front of the pick-up, and slid into the driver's seat.

Ed closed the door for her. "Lock the doors. Let me know if you see any deaders, and we'll get out of here. If I get jumped, don't wait for me."

"Are you sure?"

"Yes."

Ed headed over to the National Guard truck. It had been parked with the driver's door away from the road. He circled around back, checking the rear to make sure no deaders were hiding in there, then moved to the end and scanned the other side. Not seeing any danger, Ed moved down the side and opened the driver's door.

An arm fell through the opening. Ed jumped back and aimed his AK-47, then realized it wasn't a deader. He moved closer. The corpse of a National Guard officer sat behind the wheel, a chunk of flesh torn out of his left arm, the back of his head and brains splattered across the rear of the cab from a self-inflicted wound. Ed pulled out the body, dropped it to the ground, and climbed in.

He doubted these types of vehicles required an ignition key. Now, he only needed to figure out how to do it. He pressed the START button to the lower right of the steering column. Nothing happened. Scanning the dashboard, he noticed a T-handle knob to the left of the column with the words ENG STOP emblazoned on it. He pushed it in, then flipped into the ON position the switch to its right that read ACCESORIES. The sound of flowing fluids filled the cab. Ed waited a few seconds before pressing the START button again. The engine stuttered but would not turn over. He tried it again with the same result.

"Come on, you son of a bitch. Work."

On the third try, the engine turned over.

Ed tapped the steering wheel. "Good girl."

The drive gear was manual. It had been quite a while since he had driven a standard. Using the clutch and the stick shift, he pulled it forward seven feet, which was all he needed.

Shifting back into PARK and leaving the engine running, Ed climbed out and returned to the RAM, motioning for Lisa to roll down the window.

"You got it working."

"Finally. Pull the pick-up onto Skyline Drive. If any deaders show up, I'll use the truck to block the road. At least it'll give us a head start."

"What about the others?"

Ed turned toward Front Royal. "I hope they make it out."

PAUL SPED DOWN Main Street with the pack of deaders close behind. Daphne compared the roads around them with the map so they did not get lost, or worse, trapped in a dead end. Akiko and Toshii stared out the rear window, keeping an eye on the living dead.

Paul turned right at Cloud Street, the first one he came to, then left a few hundred feet later onto East Jackson Street, which passed through a residential neighborhood. As he made the second turn, he noticed the deaders had just entered Cloud Street. He gunned it, putting as much distance as possible between them and the pack.

"Tell me when you spot the deaders."

Several seconds later, the pack emerged onto East Jackson Street, still chasing the Pilot.

"They're behind us," warned Akiko.

Paul passed two streets before swerving right onto Blue Ridge Avenue, then pushed his foot down on the accelerator.

Daphne switched her gaze between the map and the roads around her. "I sure hope you know what you're doing."

"Trust me."

Two streets later, he swung right onto East Prospect, the tires screeching in protest.

"Any signs of them?"

Akiko shook her head. "I think we lost them."

"Let's make sure it stays that way." Paul steered the Pilot left into another residential neighborhood.

"Take your next right onto Laurel Street. That'll bring us out onto 340."

Paul followed Daphne's directions. A minute later, he turned left onto 340 and pumped his fist in the air. Daphne mumbled, "Thank God."

The road was clear except for a few vehicles parked on the sides and a row of orange traffic cones long since shoved out of the way. A few hundred feet ahead of them, a sign sat on the right side of the road with a giant arrow pointing left that read Skyline Drive.

Daphne clasped Paul's hand. "You did it."

ED SAW THE SUV pull out of one of the side streets in town and head south. Stepping into the center of the road, he waved his hands over his head to catch their attention.

AKIKO LEANED FORWARD and pointed ahead of them. "Isn't that Ed waving to us?"

"It is." Paul turned the headlights on and off several times to let their friend know they had seen him.

"I thought you were going to get lost back there," teased

Daphne.

Paul grinned. "I'd think by now you'd know me enough—"

"To your left!" shouted Toshii.

The seventy deaders chasing Ed's pick-up poured into the intersection. Paul accelerated and swerved to avoid them, barely missing running into the pack. Seven of them slammed into the side of the SUV, one getting its torn open chest caught on the side mirror. The Pilot dragged it for several yards before the mirror ripped from its mount, tossing the deader onto the road. It tripped several of the living dead, which jumped back to their feet and gave chase.

"SHIT!"

Ed unslung the AK-47, switched it to semi-automatic mode, and prepared to fire. He only had one spare magazine and did not want to waste bullets until the pack got closer.

When the SUV came within range, Ed frantically waved to the right. Paul turned onto Skyline Drive and parked alongside the RAM.

Ed emptied the entire magazine into the oncoming pack, taking down seven with headshots. When the slide stuck in the empty position, he fell back to the deuce-and-a-half, switching out the magazines as he ran.

PAUL AND DAPHNE jumped out of the Pilot. Before going to help Ed, he leaned back into the cab.

"Akiko, take the wheel. If we get overrun, you and Toshii get out of here."

Akiko nodded and got out, taking Paul's place in the driver's seat.

Paul and Daphne headed for the truck, Paul limping because of his bruised leg. Ed had already climbed into the cab.

"What are you doing?" asked Paul.

"Blocking their path. We don't want them following us."

Ed shifted into reverse and backed up the truck, blocking the access to Skyline Drive moments before the pack arrived. The sound of dozens of rotting bodies slamming into metal accompanied the snarling.

A deader in a tattered and soiled EMT uniform stumbled along the shoulder behind the truck, emerging by the tailgate. Daphne raised the Mossberg and fired, blasting off its head. It fell over and rolled down the embankment, but another made its way around the truck.

"This won't hold them for long."

Paul limped over to the cab, leaned his Vepr against the chassis, and removed his shirt.

Daphne stared at him, dumbfounded. "What are you doing?"

"Buying us time." Removing the cap from the truck's fuel tank, Paul stuffed the shirt down the opening, shoving it as deep down as possible. "I need something to light it with."

"We don't have anything." Daphne took down the deader coming around the rear of the truck with a round to its face. "Let's get out of here while we can."

LISA WATCHED IN the rearview mirror, wondering why the others had not fallen back to their vehicles. When she saw Paul stuffing his shirt into the fuel tank, she figured out what he had planned. Leaning over, she opened the glove box and rummaged through it, finding a lighter at the bottom beneath a pile of napkins and the owner's manual.

"Stay here," she said to Judith. "I'll be right back."

"No!" The girl jumped forward and grabbed her mother's arm.

"I have to do this."

"Don't leave me."

Lisa wrapped a hand around Judith's wrist and applied

pressure until the young girl released her grip.

"That hurt!"

"I don't have time to argue," snapped Lisa. "Do as you're told."

Judith began to cry as Lisa jumped out of the van, closed the door, and brought the lighter to Paul.

ED SHOT A deader coming around the front of the deuce-and-a-half. Daphne took down a third one coming from the rear.

A female deader, half the skin and all of the hair ripped off its skull, crawled beneath the chassis, reached out, and clasped Paul by the ankle of his bruised leg. The pain was so severe he almost collapsed. Paul grabbed the edge of the wooden wall running along the bed to support himself, raised his right leg, and slammed his foot down on the deader's head. The first blow had no effect other than sending a bolt of pain up his injured leg. The second cracked its skull, stunning it. Using all his might, Paul brought his foot down hard. The deader's head burst, and it released its grip. Paul stepped back, nearly falling over from the agony in his leg.

Lisa ran up. "I have a lighter."

"Give it to me."

"No. You'll never make it away in time with your bad leg. I'll do it."

Paul started to argue, but Daphne came over. "Come on. Haul ass. I'll help you."

She threw his arm over her shoulder and helped him limp back to the Pilot.

"You go, too," Lisa ordered Ed.

"You need someone to cover you." To prove his point, Ed fired three rounds into the skull of a deader that had worked its way around the front of the truck.

Lisa flicked the flint wheel on the lighter.

No flame came out.

She flicked it again.

Still no flame.

"Fuck."

"Come on." Ed grabbed Paul's Mossberg, slung it over his shoulder, and started to fall back. "It's not going to work."

Lisa flicked it a third time. Flame shot out from the opening. She placed it against the shirt.

A fourth deader circled around the rear of the truck. Ed lined up on its forehead, pulled the trigger, and blew off the back of its skull. It crumpled to the pavement, temporarily blocking the others.

"Come on."

"Give me a few more seconds," demanded Lisa.

"We don't have a few more seconds." Ed took down a deader moving around the front of the truck.

The shirt caught fire. Lisa waited a few seconds, falling back once certain the flames would not go out.

"Let's go."

"Right behind you."

Ed and Lisa retreated to the RAM.

PAUL AND DAPHNE reached the Pilot. Daphne opened the rear door.

"Get in."

"I'll drive," Paul said through a grimace.

"We don't have time to switch out." Akiko spoke in an unusually authoritative tone. "Now get in."

Daphne shoved Paul into the back, shut the door, then ran around and climbed in front.

When Daphne was safe, Akiko pulled away and headed up Skyline Drive.

ED JUMPED INTO the driver's seat of the RAM, and Lisa slid

into the front. She glanced into the side mirror. The entire shirt burned bright. What she really noticed was that five deaders had made their way around to the other side of the truck, searching for the food.

Ed pulled away and followed Akiko. The noise attracted the deaders, which broke into a run after them.

Lisa slapped Ed on the arm. "We have five deaders—"

An explosion engulfed the truck as the fuel in the gas tank ignited. The concussion rocked the vehicle. A piece of flaming steel slammed into the rear of the RAM, gouging a chunk of metal out of the tailgate. Other debris, including body parts, rained down. Ed swerved around them to prevent the tires from being punctured.

Three of the deaders chasing them had been torn apart by the blast. The other two continued their pursuit while doused in flames. They made it only a few yards before the heat shriveled their leg muscles. Both fell face forward onto the pavement, thrashing around as the fire consumed their bodies. As far as Lisa could tell, no other deaders were following them.

A few seconds later, the two vehicles entered a bend in the road, leaving the carnage behind them.

They had made it through another close encounter. Lisa only hoped their luck would hold.

She looked at Judith and smiled. "See, honey. I told you everything would be all right."

Judith refused to look at her. When Lisa reached in back to take her hand, Judith slapped it away and stared out the window.

There are worse things than being eaten by deaders, Lisa thought.

Chapter Seven

THE GROUP STOPPED at the Dicky Ridge Visitor Center, five miles along Skyline Drive. Paul wanted to make sure that the group was okay and that the Pilot and RAM had not suffered any critical damage, which they had not. Thankfully, they did not suffer any casualties. Since the area seemed secure, with no abandoned vehicles or signs of deader activity, Paul told everyone to rest for ten minutes before moving out.

Daphne crossed the road to the overlook across from the visitor center. The sun cast its rays upon the Shenandoah Valley, highlighting the foliage. The beautiful view reminded her of a Normal Rockwell portrait, with green, red, orange, and yellow mixed together, painting the surrounding slopes in a natural beauty. For a few seconds, Daphne forgot about the nightmare engulfing the world. Then her gaze fell upon a pillar of black smoke billowing from a nearby town, slapping her back to reality.

"I'm behind you," warned Akiko as she joined Daphne. "Mind if I join you?"

"Not at all. How are you and the kids doing?"

"As well as can be expected. Gojira is a distraction for them, which is good. I'm worried whether they can emotionally and psychologically handle what we're going through. And I always wonder what type of world will be left for them a year from now."

"I'm sure Japan will find a way to make it through this."

Akiko bowed her head. "I doubt that. Over one hundred

and twenty million people live in Japan, mostly in big cities. My grandparents' generation lived through the war and the devastation of our homeland, then rebuilt the country from nothing. Today's generation is too pampered. It'll be decades before Japan recovers, if ever."

Daphne said nothing. There was nothing to say.

"It's ironic," continued Akiko. "Iso and I brought Toshii here to show him how beautiful the United States was. Who would have thought this would become our homeland?"

Daphne wrapped her arm around the woman and pulled her close. "Paul and I are glad you're here. You're welcome to stay with us as long as you want."

"Thank you." Akiko paused. "Are you and Paul an item yet?"

"What?"

"Are you two lovers yet? It's obvious to everyone the two of you love each other."

"Well… I thanked him once for saving my life."

"What you do is your own business, but I wouldn't wait too long. You never know how much time you have left. I can attest to that."

Off in the distance, the sound of gunfire broke the silence, followed by the moans of the living dead and a human scream, ruining the moment.

A whistle caught their attention. The women turned around to see everyone else getting into the vehicles. Paul waved for Daphne and Akiko to join them.

Toshii ran up to his mother. "Can me and Gojira ride with Judith?"

"I don't think so. There's not enough room for all of us in the pick-up."

"But we both want company."

"Aren't I company enough?"

"You're my mother. That doesn't count."

Ed suppressed a chuckle.

"Come on, mom." The boy was practically bouncing in place. "Please?"

Gojira joined in with a bark.

Akiko released a sigh only a mother could give and looked at Ed. "Is it okay with you?"

Ed nodded. "The kids and Gojira can sit in back. Which one of you is riding shotgun?"

"You ride with them," said Lisa. "I'll go with Paul and Daphne."

"Are you sure?"

Lisa nodded and headed for the Pilot. Akiko, Toshii, and Gojira climbed into the RAM.

Two minutes later, the group was back on the road.

THEY DROVE FOR another twenty miles, passing the Elkwallow Wayside and Picnic Grounds. Half a mile beyond that, Paul slowed. A school bus sat across the road, the rear end in their lane and the front blocking the opposite, with not enough room to maneuver around it.

"That isn't good." Daphne lifted the Mossberg off the floor.

Paul pulled over to the side of the road and stopped. "Stay here in case we need to move in a hurry."

"Gotcha."

Ed joined him at the front of the SUV. "I thought the authorities closed this road to traffic."

"Somehow, this one got through. Cover me while I check it out."

Paul and Ed moved over to the rear of the bus. Paul leaned forward and stared around the right side, expecting to see the dead feeding off bodies. There were no signs of carnage. Waving for Ed to follow, he approached the front door. It was closed, with no signs of a struggle. Pushing against the center seam, the door opened. Paul stepped onto the bus, his Vepr raised into the high-ready position, sweeping the weapon from side to side. The interior was clean—no blood, no bodies, no carnage. Lowering the shotgun, he stepped off, leaving the doors open.

"What did you find?" asked Ed.

"There are no signs of a deader attack, so hopefully, it broke down and was abandoned."

"What do we do now?"

Paul looked behind him. "We're on a slight incline, so I can roll it out of the way. Back up the vehicles a few hundred feet so I don't accidentally bump them."

"Do you want me to provide cover?"

"I'm good."

Ed nodded and returned to the vehicles.

Paul climbed back inside, slid into the driver's seat, and rested the shotgun against the dashboard. The keys were in the ignition. Turning them, the engine came to life.

"I wouldn't do that."

The voice came from behind him and nearly scared the shit out of Paul. He jumped to his feet, stumbling slightly from the pain. Grabbing the Vepr, he spun around and aimed at the rear of the bus.

A young boy about the same age as Toshii sat in the rear seat to the left of the Emergency Exit. Strawberry blonde hair hung down to his shoulder, with several strands draping across his face, which bore no emotions.

Paul lowered the Vepr a few inches but kept his finger near the trigger. "Who are you?"

"I'm Tommy." He raised his hand and waved once.

"Are you bitten?"

"No."

"Are you alone?"

"Now I am."

Paul cautiously made his way to the rear. "What are you doing here?"

"Hiding."

"How long have you been here?"

Tommy glanced at his watch. "Thirty-nine hours and twenty-seven minutes."

Tommy's expression had not changed. He didn't even seem upset that a strange man with a gun approached him. Paul swung the Vepr over his shoulder and sat in the seat across from the boy.

"I'm Paul." He offered his hand.

The boy shook it, his grip extremely weak. "Nice to meet you."

"Why didn't you say anything when I came on the first time?"

"I didn't know who you were. I thought you might be a revenant."

"A revenant?"

"Someone who has returned from the dead."

The kid may lack emotions but was intelligent beyond his years. "Why did you reach out to me the second time?"

"I knew you weren't one of them. They're not smart enough to start a school bus."

"Good point." Paul smiled. "You said you were hiding."

"I am."

"From what?"

Tommy looked out the window to his right and pointed. "Them."

Chapter Eight

THREE DEADERS EMERGED from the woods. The male wore jeans and a t-shirt, both soaked in dried blood, the shirt bottom in tatters. Its abdominal cavity had been cleaned out. Two female deaders followed close behind. The taller of the two, dressed in jeans and a flannel shirt, had its left arm torn off, the broken humerus protruding beneath the shredded sleeve. The other wore a sundress. It limped onto the road, trying to steady itself on the base of the tibia where its right foot was missing.

The footless deader, on detecting the Pilot's engine, sauntered toward the rear of the bus.

The other female stood in place, lifting its head and sniffing, trying to figure out if it should go toward the noise or the scent of fresh meat.

The male deader stumbled up the stairs to the bus and stopped, hovering over the steering wheel.

Tommy tapped Paul on the arm and motioned for him to lean over. When Paul did, Tommy whispered, "That's the bus driver."

Spinning toward the rear of the bus, the deader snarled and attacked.

"WHAT'S TAKING HIM so long?" Daphne asked in a soft voice.

"Give him time," said Lisa. "He's probably never driven anything so… shit."

The limping deader emerged from the side of the bus and stumbled toward their SUV.

"I got this." Lisa opened the door and stepped out, using it as a shield. She aimed the AK-47 and fired a single round. The deader's head shot back as the bullet struck between its eyes and exited out the back, tearing away chunks of skull and brains.

A few seconds later, a female deader with no left arm ran around the bus and charged Lisa. She aimed and fired two rounds. The first struck its shoulder, causing minimal damage. The second caught it in the face, blowing off the top of its head. It crumbled ten feet from Lisa.

Daphne jumped out of the front seat. "I have to check on Paul."

Before she could move, four more deaders emerged from the woods—two females, a male in hunter's gear, and a National Guardsman. Upon spotting Daphne and Lisa, they lunged.

PAUL UNSLUNG THE Vepr from his shoulder. Before he could aim, the deader slammed into him, pinning the weapon between their bodies. Paul used the shotgun to push back against the deader, but it did little good. Its face hovered inches from Paul's, snapping at the fresh meat.

ED EXITED THE RAM, closed the door, and raised his AK-47.

"Hey!"

The call startled the four deaders, which paused their attack. Ed and Lisa took down the two female deaders with well-placed headshots. Daphne circled around the front of the SUV and fired at the hunter deader, blasting away its lower jaw and spine. Its head tilted at an obscene angle. Before the body hit the asphalt, Daphne switched aim to the National Guardsman and fired. The round shattered its skull.

AKIKO NOTICED MOVEMENT in her side mirror. A second National Guardsman emerged from the woods behind them. It had no face. Its upper jaw and nasal cavity had been blasted apart, leaving a gaping hole. The lower jaw was missing, allowing its tattered tongue to hang onto its neck. Its eyes had been dislodged from their sockets, dangling over the open wound. Because of its injuries, the deader had no clue where to go and stumbled around aimlessly, attempting to home in on the gunfire.

Akiko stepped out of the RAM, pausing long enough to lean back inside.

"Lock the doors and stay inside no matter what happens. Understood?"

Toshii and Judith both nodded. Gojira barked.

The barking attracted the faceless deader, which stumbled toward them.

Akiko raised the AK-47. Never having fired a weapon before, she had set it for three-round bursts. The first rounds tore into its chest and neck, severing the dangling tongue. She took a deep breath, adjusted her aim, and fired again. All three rounds struck in the exposed nasal cavity, tearing off what little remained on its head.

More rustling came from the trees. Daphne and the others moved to the center of the road and raised their weapons. A moment later, the first deader appeared.

Ed lowered his AK-47. "Fuck, no!"

THE BUS DRIVER deader pushed against Paul, its mouth getting dangerously close to his neck. Paul released his grip on the Vepr and used his hands to push back the deader's chin, saving himself from being bit. The shotgun clattered to the floor.

Moving his hands down to the deader's neck, Paul grabbed its collar and pushed forward, knocking it off balance. Paul let go and shoved. The deader toppled onto the floor.

Turning around, Paul ran back to the Emergency Exit to get his weapon. Tommy already had it and aimed at the thing.

"Duck, please."

Two shots rang through the bus with a deafening sound. The first caught the deader in the chest as it struggled onto its feet. The second tore off its left arm, causing the deader to collapse face-first onto the floor.

Paul took the shotgun from Tommy, went back to the deader, and fired a single round into the back of its head. Congealed blood and gore splattered up the walls and across the ceiling.

"Thanks, kid."

"See, we're not useless."

"I never said you were."

That was when Paul heard the barrage of gunfire from outside.

ED LOWERED HIS AK-47. "Fuck, no!"

Seven child deaders emerged from the tree line. The oldest was a boy around eleven, the youngest a girl no more than four. Golden locks flowed down the right side of its head but not on the right, which had been chewed off. It clutched a blood-soaked teddy bear against its chest. They stopped at the edge of the road and stared at the humans as if uncertain what to do. The teddy bear deader twitched its head and focused its milky gaze on Daphne.

Daphne lowered the barrel of her Mossberg a few inches. "I can't."

As one, the deaders snarled and attacked.

They did not get far.

Akiko and Lisa opened fire, spraying the living dead with

rapid, three-round bursts. A crimson mist formed behind the child deaders, mixed in with chunks of gore. Three were brought down immediately with headshots, their tiny bodies dropping to the asphalt. Two more fell halfway to the humans. The older boy proved harder to stop, taking two three-round bursts in the chest and head from Akiko and Lisa before it staggered and fell onto the road.

Lisa turned and fired three shots at the little girl about to lunge at Daphne. One round missed. One punched into its shoulder, knocking it off balance. The third struck its neck, severing the spine. The girl deader went limp, releasing the gore-covered teddy bear, then collapsed in front of Daphne.

Akiko switched to single-shot mode and walked down the line of living dead, putting a single round into the back of each head.

As Akiko ensured the living dead were put out of their misery, Daphne approached the little girl deader. Its head lay on the ground at an angle, with the teddy bear beside it. The deader focused its gaze on Daphne, the white orbs devoid of all life or emotion, the little mouth biting the air. Daphne stared at it, unable to respond, fighting back the disgust raging inside her.

Akiko stepped up, switched out her empty magazine with a fresh one, then fired a single round between its eyes, turning the once sweet face into a pile of goo.

"Are you two okay?" asked Lisa.

Ed remained silent.

Daphne finally diverted her attention from the body and made eye contact with Lisa.

"They… they were just children."

"These things are the living dead, what we in Japan call *shinde ikiru*," replied Akiko. She pointed to Toshii and Julie in the pick-up. "They're children. We did what we had to to save them."

Daphne lowered her head. She had let emotions get the

better of her. If not for Akiko and Lisa, she would be dead by now, or been bitten and condemned to damnation.

Ed changed the subject. "Where's Paul?"

"Right here." He walked around the rear of the bus accompanied by a young boy. "Everyone, this is Tommy. He saved my life on the bus."

Daphne ran over, dropped to her knees, and hugged Tommy.

Paul smiled at the display of affection. "We better get before any more of those things show up."

"There are no more," said Tommy. "There were fifteen in total. My classmates. Miss Calpin and her aides. The driver. The two National Guardsmen. And the guy who started it all. We should be safe now."

"Even so, I want to hit the road in case the gunfire attracts other deaders nearby. Tommy, for now, you'll ride with me. Let's move out while we have the chance."

Chapter Nine

THE CONVOY DROVE for a few miles before Lisa offered her hand to Tommy. "By the way, I'm Lisa. The woman up front is Daphne."

He shook it, giving the hand a dramatic pump. "I'm Tommy."

"You were lucky to survive."

"The kid's smart," said Paul from the driver's seat.

"My parents don't think I'm smart. I just used common sense. Once the adults started to turn and Miss Calpin led the others into the woods, the only rational thing to do was stay on the bus where it was safe."

Daphne shifted in her seat to look at Tommy. "What happened?"

"We were in school when the outbreak began. Miss Calpin's School for the Gifted."

"Gifted?" asked Daphne.

"We are… were… autistic. My parents were embarrassed by that, always telling me I was born dumber than most kids."

"You're not," said Paul.

"I know. But they didn't see it that way. In any case, most parents came to pick up their kids on the first day of the outbreak. As for the rest of us, well… ours never showed up. We assumed they were either dead or unable to reach us because of the confusion. We spent the first night in the school, but no one came for us. In the morning, the dead were overrunning Front Royal, so Miss Calpin decided to get us somewhere safe. Miss Calpin's husband was with us. He knew how to drive a bus, so we took the one the school used for field trips and fled the city."

"How did you wind up on Skyline Drive?" asked Lisa.

"Mr. Calpin thought it would be the safest way out of the city. A couple of National Guardsmen had blocked the road with a truck. Mrs. Calpin knew one of them and convinced him it was the best way to get us somewhere safe. The Guardsman agreed and let us through. We would have made it if it wasn't for those two bad men.

"We came across two more Guardsmen arguing with two guys in a Jeep dressed like hunters. The Jeep blocked the road. They were arguing with the Guardsmen about something. Mr. Calpin stopped the bus and asked if they could move the Jeep so we could pass. One of the Guardsmen began arguing with Mr. Calpin. That's when one of the hunters shot the other Guardsman in the face with a shotgun and then the one arguing with Mr. Calpin in the chest. They then began arguing with Mr. Calpin.

"That's when the two Guardsmen reanimated and attacked Mr. Calpin and one of the hunters. The second hunter jumped into his Jeep and drove off. Mrs. Calpin went out to help her husband and was attacked by the dead. The aides got everyone else off the bus and headed into the woods."

"But you stayed behind," said Daphne.

"It was the smart… the commonsense thing to do. I had been watching the news at school and knew those who turned were fast, and that the others didn't stand a chance. I hid at the rear of the bus, hoping those things would not come back. If they did and somehow got onto the bus, I could escape out the Emergency Exit."

"How long were you there?" asked Lisa.

"Since yesterday morning. When Paul got on, I stayed hidden in case he was one of them. Then I heard him talking to you. Deaders don't talk, so I let him know I was there when he came back on board."

"It's a good thing he was," added Paul. "The kid saved my life. Thanks."

"You're welcome."

"You're safe with us," said Daphne. "We'll take care of you."

"Thank you, Miss Daphne."

Lisa reached over to hug him, then stopped. "When we stop for the night, I'll introduce you to my daughter, Judith, and Toshii. They're about your age."

"I'm eleven."

Daphne grinned. "We'll also introduce you to Gojira."

Tommy looked at the three adults, a confused expression on his face. "You have a giant monster with you?"

Daphne chuckled. "That's what Toshii named the dog we picked up on the way."

"I love dogs. My parents would never let me have a pet. They said I was too irresponsible."

AFTER DRIVING FOR another two hours, the group reached Rockfish Gap Station, the last stop at the opposite end of Skyline Drive. Paul parked in front of the entrance station, turned off the engine, and stepped out of the vehicle. Fingers loudly scratched against glass. Paul raised the Mossberg, his attention drawn to the station. A deader in a Park Ranger uniform scraped at the station door window, banging on or gnawing at the glass every few seconds. It snarled repeatedly, the sound muffled by being inside. Paul considered putting the thing out of its misery, opting against it. Why waste ammo or draw more attention to themselves?

Ed parked behind him and turned off the engine. Everyone gathered around the front of the SUV, including Gojira and the children. The latter introduced each other and played with the dog as the adults looked down Skyline Drive, wondering what awaited them.

"Where do we go from here?" asked Lisa.

"Hang on." Daphne unfolded and refolded the map until she found the correct page. "Here we are. According to this, Skyline Drive merges with I-64 in a rural area. Charlottesville is about twenty east of us. A couple of miles to the west are Waynesboro, Lyndhurst, Stuart's Draft, Fishersville, and Staunton."

Ed shook his head. "Neither option sounds good."

"What's to the south?" asked Akiko.

"Back roads running through farmland." Daphne folded the map and slid it under her arm. "That's our best route out of here."

"Then what?" asked Lisa. "Where do we go once clear of this area?"

"That's what we have to decide," Paul answered. "Our best chance of survival is heading for a part of the country that's lightly populated and will have less of the living dead to contend with. We can head west to Arizona and New Mexico or north to Wyoming and the Dakotas. I prefer heading north."

"What's up north?" asked Akiko.

"Snow."

"And that's a selling point?" joked Ed.

"It is for stopping deaders. Winter is only a month away. Once the snow hits, it'll be so deep it'll bury the deaders and freeze them, making it safer for us to move around. That will give us plenty of time to set up a compound to ride this out. The downside is it'll be a miserable winter since we're unprepared. We'll have to find cold weather gear, several months of supplies, and a heated place to fortify. Once the good weather starts, we'll be able to police the area for miles around and kill any deaders that are still frozen, which will make it a lot easier in the spring. Assuming we make it to the spring."

"So much for a winter wonderland." Lisa frowned. "What are the pros and cons of heading west?"

Paul contemplated his answer for a moment. "We don't have to worry about surviving winter. But we still have to find a place to fortify and stock up while doing that under the constant threat of deader activity."

"Won't there be fewer deaders in the desert than here?" asked Lisa.

"In the beginning. We should be safe for a year or two so long as we stay away from major cities. But there is the possibility that when the food supply in major population areas dries up, the dead may start migrating west. It'll be a lot harder to defend ourselves in the desert. Ideally, I'd like to set up camp in the Rockies, but they're two-thirds of the way across the country."

Daphne sighed. "You're saying our choice is being killed by either the weather or the living dead."

"I was trying to be a bit more optimistic, but yes."

An uncomfortable silence fell over the group.

Ed spoke first. "Is there anything else new we should consider before we vote?"

Tommy joined them. "Our chances of making it north are twice as good than if we head west."

"Why do you say that?" asked Pual.

"To make it New Mexico, we'll have to go through Nashville, Atlanta, Chattanooga, or Birmingham. Once we clear that, we still must drive through Dallas-Fort Worth or Oklahoma City."

"We can just drive around them, can't we?" asked Lisa.

"We could." Daphne shook her head. But to avoid the major cities and suburbs would add hundreds of miles to our trip and keep us exposed that much longer."

"And that many more supply runs," added Paul, remembering the nightmare at FedEx.

Tommy jumped back in. "And we'll have to find a way to

cross the Mississippi River. Most of the crossings are in big cities."

Daphne sighed. "We got to assume the authorities blew up most of them to contain the outbreak."

"No, no." Akiko shook her head. "Even if they didn't destroy them, we'd never make it through the city."

"And it could take us days to find a crossing," added Ed.

Tommy continued talking as if he had not been interrupted. "If we go northwest, there are still several big cities to pass through or around–Cincinnati, Columbus, Indianapolis, Des Moines, and Minneapolis. But the Mississippi River ends in Minneapolis. There are no rivers to cross. Once we pass Minneapolis, the roads to Wyoming and North Dakota open up."

The adults looked at Tommy dumbfounded.

"How do you know all this?" asked Ed.

"I like geography."

"Good job, kid." Paul smiled, patted Tommy on the shoulder, and then turned to the others. "Any objections heading north?"

No one objected.

"All right. We move out in ten minutes."

Chapter Ten

EXITING SKYLINE DRIVE, the group crossed under I-84 and proceeded for half an hour along Blue Ridge Drive before turning onto Tye River Turnpike. Both roads wound through the woods and, fortunately, were devoid of traffic or the living dead except for an occasional car abandoned along the side or a lone deader.

As they came to the end of the turnpike, Paul pointed ahead of them to a populated area. Twin overpasses sat a mile ahead of them.

"What's that?"

Daphne consulted the map. "Raphine. That overpass is I-64/I-81. I don't think we should risk it."

"I'm not. But we're running low on gas. Just under a quarter of a tank. Where's the nearest town after this?"

Daphne unfolded the map. "There's nothing until after we make our way through the foothills and enter West Virginia."

"Let's hope we find a gas station soon."

The two vehicles drew closer to town. Daphne tapped Paul's leg and pointed ahead. A large Exxon sign stood beyond the trees.

"We're in luck."

"Maybe," said Paul. "As long as it's not overrun."

Daphne smiled when they passed the tree line and entered the gas station. It was deserted. She gently nudged him on the arm.

"You never listen to me."

Paul ignored the jab. He pulled up to the farthest pump and parked, leaving the engine running, then turned to Daphne and grinned.

"Same procedure as last time?"

Daphne leaned over and kissed him on the cheek. "You're a lousy date. You make me pay for everything."

She climbed out of the Pilot. Ed pulled up on the opposite side of the pumps.

"Everything okay?" he asked.

"We're refilling while we have a chance." Daphne swiped her credit card and entered her PIN. "Paul and I have less than a quarter of a tank. How are you set?"

Ed glanced at the fuel gauge. "Half a tank."

"Let's fill you up, too."

Daphne inserted the nozzle into the inlet pipe and began pumping gas, then crossed over to the RAM and swiped her card through his pump. When the card was approved, Ed started filling his tank.

"I hope you have good credit," joked Ed. "I don't want to run out of gas halfway to Wyoming."

Akiko leaned forward. "I'm afraid the electricity will run out before your card does."

"Shit, I hadn't thought about that." Daphne thought for a moment. "Akiko, come with me."

"Can we go, too?" asked Toshii.

"No." Akiko glared at Toshii and Judith. "You stay here. Understood?"

They both nodded.

As they passed by Paul, Daphne said, "We're going to check out the station for any gas cans to take with us. Don't shut down the pump until we get back."

"Be careful."

Daphne smiled. "I always am."

The Exxon was a combination gas station/convenience store. Akiko peered through the window. The place had been ransacked. The coolers, freezers, and shelves had been picked clean, with anything not of survival value tossed onto the floor. The cash register drawers stood open, the trays empty. She found it sadly amusing that the cigarette racks had also been emptied.

Akiko knocked on the glass.

Nothing.

She opened the door and called out, "Is anyone here?"

No response.

Akiko turned to Daphne. "It's clear."

"I THINK WE should help Mom," suggested Toshii as he stared at the station. "We might find something useful in there."

Judith shook her head several times. "Your mother told us not to."

"She's being overcautious."

"I don't want your mother getting—"

Gojira stuck his head between the two kids, his ears back, his attention focused on the windshield. The dog growled. Toshii reached up and rubbed the dog's head.

"What's wrong, boy?"

Judith motioned with her head. "That."

A thousand feet ahead of them, a single deader stumbled off the exit ramp to I-81 and slowly crossed the road, wandering aimlessly. Six more followed behind it. It reminded Toshii of that time in the park when he watched a dozen pigeons milling about looking for food.

Toshii gently tapped the glass to get Ed's attention, then pointed in front of them. Ed looked and mumbled the "F" word.

THE WOMEN SEARCHED the station until Akiko found three red plastic containers on a section of the wall against the rear of the store displaying auto supplies. It had not been touched. She waved Daphne over.

"Will these do?"

"Those are perfect." Daphne handed one to Akiko and took the other two. "Let's go."

ED LEANED AROUND the pump and snapped his fingers. When Paul looked at him, Ed raised a finger to his lips and then pointed toward the small pack of deaders. Paul's eyes widened for a second, then the prepper attitude returned. He gave Ed the thumbs up.

Both men listened for the sound of gasoline flowing up the inlet pipe, shutting off the nozzles manually to avoid the loud clicking of the automatic shut-off. Ed replaced the nozzle, put the cap back on the tank, screwed it on, silently closed the panel, and waited by the driver's door.

Paul left the nozzle in the tank and cautiously made his way toward the store section of the gas station. He got there as Daphne and Akiko exited.

Daphne raised the two containers over her head. Before she could speak, Paul ran his fingers back and forth across his neck, then motioned with his head down the road. The two women became quiet when they spotted the deaders and slowly followed Paul back to the pumps.

Daphne removed the nozzle from the Pilot's tank and used it to begin filling the first container. Paul quietly opened the SUV's rear hatch. Akiko unslung her AK-47 in case they had to fight their way out and stood by the passenger door to the RAM.

When the first container was full, Daphne switched it out with an empty one, not bothering to turn off the nozzle. Paul screwed on the cap, carried it over to the RAM, and placed it in the bed.

The seven deaders continued stumbling across the road.

Gojira growled even louder. Toshii slid his hands up the dog's face and clasped his jaw shut. Judith rubbed Gojira's back.

When the second container was full, Daphne switched it out with the last empty one. Paul sealed it up and brought it to the back of their SUV, moving a few boxes aside to fit in the gas can. One of the boxes fell over, almost tumbling out of the rear deck. Paul pushed his shoulder against it, holding it in place. Seeing what happened, Daphne left the nozzle in the container and rushed over to help.

Ed kept an eye on the pack. They still meandered across the street.

Akiko raised the AK-47 just in case.

Daphne grabbed the box and whispered for Paul to move his shoulder. He did. Daphne returned the box to its position and held it in place while Paul put in the gas can.

"Thanks," he whispered.

"That's what I'm here for. To save your ass."

At that moment, the gas container reached maximum capacity, and the nozzle automatically shut off with a loud click.

The seven deaders swung around to face the Exxon station, snarled, and charged.

Akiko raised her AK-47 and fired a three-round burst, striking the lead deader in the abdomen and chest. The gunfire barely slowed it down. She switched to semi-automatic mode and kept pulling the trigger, emptying the entire magazine, succeeding in bringing down only two of the living dead. Akiko switched out magazines.

Ed removed the nozzle, dropped it on the ground, and closed the tank. Using the driver's door as a shield, he fired on the pack, taking out one deader with two rounds to the head.

"Forget them," Daphne yelled to Ed and Akiko from the back of the Pilot. "Get inside where it's safe. We'll be ready in a few seconds."

Ed and Akiko obeyed, jumping back into the RAM and

closing the doors.

Daphne slammed shut the hatch and turned to Paul. "That goes for you, too."

"What about you?"

"I'll be right behind you."

Paul limped to the door. The remaining four deaders still rushed toward the gas station, now only two hundred feet away. He aimed the Vepr and fired but was too far away for the rounds to do anything more than punch holes into dead flesh. Sliding into the driver's seat, he shifted into DRIVE, waiting for Daphne.

Daphne yanked the nozzle out of the container, tossed it aside, screwed on the cap, shoved the gas can in the back deck, and closed the hatch. She ran forward and jumped into the passenger's seat, closing the door behind her, then checked to see how close the deaders were.

"Fuck."

Paul looked ahead of him and agreed with Daphne.

The four surviving deaders were only a hundred feet away. They were not the problem. The gunfire had attracted every other deader in Raphine, especially those wandering among the traffic on I-84. More than a thousand of the living dead poured down the ramps from the highway, with a few hundred more racing down the road from the town center. They would be overwhelmed within seconds.

"Hang on!"

Paul stomped his foot on the accelerator. The Pilot bolted forward, fishtailing out of the gas station and heading straight into the horde. Ed pulled away and fell in behind, maintaining the same speed at a distance of twenty feet.

Merging into the right lane, Paul swerved around the three closest deaders. The fourth lunged, slamming into the SUV's left front fender and being thrown aside. Paul headed for the entrance ramp onto I-84 East.

"What are you doing?" asked Lisa. "We'll never escape that way."

"Trust me."

The mass of deaders swarmed into the right lane and converged on the two vehicles, now only thirty feet away.

Daphne glanced over and calmly asked, "Paul?"

Paul spun the steering wheel. The Pilot swerved left, entering the opposite lane and racing past the bulk of the rampaging horde. The right fender of the SUV clipped several deaders, throwing them back into the others. One of the living dead, its hands cuffed behind its back, bounced off the hood and hit the windshield. A crack spider-webbed across the glass. The body rolled onto the roof and fell to the wayside.

Paul increased speed, ramming those in front of them out of the way and praying none got lodged beneath the chassis.

"DAMN IT."

Caught off guard, Ed did not veer off until two seconds later. The right fender of the RAM cut through the outer rim of the horde, knocking a score of deaders over like bowling pins. Those they passed swung around and gave chase. Dozens either ran in front of the pick-up or bounced off the right side of the vehicle. Gojira barked. Toshii leaned away from the window. Judith tried to remain stoic.

Akiko lodged the AK-47 between the floor and the center console, then shifted in her seat to face Toshii.

"Give me your handgun."

He passed it to his mother. "Why do you need it?"

"In case any of them break through the windows." Akiko shifted in her seat so that she faced the side windows.

Ed swung in behind and a few feet to the left of the SUV, staying close to Paul and letting him clear the path.

THE LIVING DEAD closed in on three sides. Paul kept his foot pressed on the accelerator, but the gathering mass of dead gradually slowed the Pilot's speed. If the horde of deaders in front of them stopped their momentum, this would be where everyone died.

Daphne sensed the growing tension. "Will we make it?"

"I'm not sure."

Daphne reloaded her Mossberg. If they became trapped, she would ensure none of them lived long enough to be turned.

Lisa noticed Daphne loading rounds into the Mossberg, knowing what she intended and agreeing with her. She wished she had stayed with Judith so she could comfort her daughter through this. Instead, she held Tommy's hand, as much for her sake as his.

"It'll be okay."

"I know. I trust you, Paul, and Daphne."

Paul swore under his breath as the SUV slowed to twenty-five miles per hour.

"BUCKLE UP," ED warned the two kids in back.

"Why?"

"Just do as I say."

A state trooper in a motorcycle helmet, the lower half of his face eaten away, rammed its head against the passenger window. The glass shattered, covering Akiko in shards. The momentum of the RAM prevented it from crawling inside. Instead, its jaw lodged against the rear rim of the window, the rest of its body being dragged along. Akiko tried to shove it out, but it would not budge. Grabbing the deader's helmet, she pushed up and out. The jaw snapped off, falling into the back seat. The deader tumbled off the RAM.

Before Akiko could get her hands back inside, a female deader in a gore-encrusted jogging outfit clutched her right arm and attacked. Akiko grabbed the deader's ponytail with her left hand and pulled the head to the side, preventing it from biting her. The decayed scalp began to pull away from its skull.

Ed veered right back into the mass of living dead. An overweight deader in a yellow road worker's vest ran into the door, tearing off the side mirror and tripping the jogger deader. It fell to the ground, releasing its grip on Akiko.

She picked up the revolver from the seat and aimed it at the window, ready to eliminate the next thing that tried to crawl through.

THE PILOT HAD passed beneath both overpasses for I-84, having slowed to nine miles per hour.

It suddenly broke through the horde onto the open road and accelerated forward. For a moment, Paul lost control of the vehicle. He slowed long enough to regain control, then pushed down on the gas pedal. The SUV pulled away from the horde.

Paul checked his rearview mirror. Ed had broken out of the mass of living dead and was ten feet behind him. The horde still pursued them but rapidly fell behind.

"We got problems." Daphne motioned with her head toward the dashboard.

The engine temperature light shone bright red. Busting their way through the horde must have damaged the radiator. Paul hoped they could keep going long enough to put considerable distance between them and the living dead.

Thankfully, Rapine was a small town, and most of the living dead congregated along the highway where the food was. A few dozen deaders wandered ahead of them, but few enough and spread out so Paul could easily maneuver around them. A few minutes later, they had passed through the town and were on Route 606, heading through a wooded area.

Paul slowed. He drove until he reached the intersection with Brownsburg Turnpike, took a left, and pulled over to the side of the road. Daphne climbed out to check on the engine.

Ed parked off to the side of the road. He and Akiko exited

and came up alongside them. "What's wrong?"

"We damaged the radiator back there." Paul opened the door and stepped out. "I'm hoping we can fix it. Otherwise, we'll have to ride with you until we find another vehicle."

"That may not be an issue." Daphne stood in front of the SUV and waved for Paul to join her. Ed and Akiko followed.

A deader in a National Guard uniform was lodged in the Pilot's grill, held in place by its utility belt and the fingers of its right hand entwined in the air vents. The legs had been torn off in the melee. Pieces of flesh and muscle dangled from where the limbs had ripped away, with clots of congealed blood dripping onto the road. It twisted its head toward Paul and snarled.

"Fucking awesome." Toshii stood behind Paul, staring at the mangled deader.

"Watch your language," snapped Akiko. "And what are you doing out here?"

Toshii pointed to Gojira who crouched on the other side of the road, relieving himself.

Judith ran over and hugged her mother.

"Are you alright?" asked Lisa.

"I was scared."

"But she didn't show it," said Toshii. "She was very brave."

Tommy came around the front of the SUV and stood between Paul and Daphne, showing no emotion. "We'll see worse before this is over."

Even though he did not want to admit it, Paul knew the kid was right.

He leaned over to pull the deader off. "Let's get rid of this thing and hit the road."

It snapped at him, forcing Paul to jump back. Akiko stepped forward and put a single round through its skull, the burst sending a swarm of flies and wasps airborne. The deader went limp. Congealed blood, gore, and maggots splattered across the hood. Akiko moved away and nodded to proceed.

Paul and Ed dislodged the carcass from the grill, carried it over to the shoulder, tossed it aside, and cleaned off their hands in the grass.

"What now?" asked Lisa.

Daphne checked her watch. "It's almost four. The sun will be going down soon."

Paul avoided the insects that settled on the human detritus covering the hood. "We need to find a safe place to settle down for the night."

The group got back into their vehicles and continued down Brownsburg Turnpike.

Chapter Eleven

THE SAFE PLACE they came across was several miles down the road shortly after Brownsburg Turnpike changed into Maury River Road. Off to the right stood an old, two-story motel. The entrances to the rooms were on the exterior of the building connected on each floor by covered walkways, which meant they would not have to venture inside to find a place to sleep. That significantly decreased the danger of running into a pack of the living dead hidden inside the motel or trapped in their rooms. However, what attracted their attention most was that the parking lot remained vacant except for one car parked in the customer drop-off area, and there were no corpses or signs of a struggle.

Paul pulled into the parking lot and stopped along the right side of the building. Ed drove up alongside him and rolled down the driver's window.

"What do you think?" asked Paul.

"It looks safe enough. But...."

"I know what you mean. Stay here. If you see any deaders, continue for two miles and wait for us."

"What are you going to do?"

"See if there's anything to worry about."

Paul cruised down the lot to the end of the motel, shifted into neutral, revved the engine for five seconds, then shifted back into drive. Nothing emerged from the surrounding trees or from inside the hotel. He continued the same procedure along the rear, left, and front of the motel. When finished, he pulled up beside the RAM.

"See anything?" asked Ed.

"Just a pack of squirrels near the dumpster that ran like hell when we went by."

"What now?"

"We check each room to make certain no surprises are waiting for us, then we'll see if there are any keys left. You and Daphne check out the rooms on this side. Akiko and I will do the other. That way, each group has a shotgun."

"How will we get in without the keys?" asked Akiko.

"Don't take the risk. Knock on the doors or windows and see if you get a response."

"If we do?" The question came from Daphne.

"If it's one or two deaders, we clear them out. If the place is crawling, we move on." Paul glanced at the others. "Any questions?"

No one had any.

"Send the kids and Gojira over to us. If this thing goes south, Lisa can get the kids to safety." Paul shifted in his seat to check with Lisa. "Is that okay with you?"

"Sure."

"Let's do this."

Toshii, Judith, and Gojira switched vehicles. Lisa slid into the driver's seat and locked the doors.

Paul and Akiko entered the crossway between the rooms on the first floor and the lobby, pausing in front of the entrance to the laundry room. He stayed to the right and motioned for Akiko to knock. She gently tapped her knuckles twice on the door.

"You'll have to do it louder."

"Sorry." This time, she pounded the bottom of her fist on it three times.

No sounds came from inside.

Paul raised the Vepr. "See if it opens."

Akiko grabbed the knob and turned. The latch clicked. She

pushed the door open and jumped back out of the line of fire. Nothing attacked them. Paul moved closer and peered inside. It was empty. He closed the door, and they proceeded around the corner to the rooms.

The curtains of the first one were pulled aside, allowing them to see in. Paul watched as Akiko pounded on the door. Nothing stirred.

"Do it again."

Akiko pounded a second time with the same results.

As they moved down to the next room, Paul scanned the parking lot to make sure no deaders approached from the woods.

This one had the curtains drawn. Paul leaned closer to the glass so he could hear inside. Akiko pounded on the door, waited a few seconds, then pounded again. Silence.

"Is the door unlocked?" asked Paul.

Akiko tried it and shook her head.

The two performed the same routine on each room along the first floor, finding nothing, then moved up to the second level.

DAPHNE AND ED ran the same procedures along the first floor on the right side of the motel without finding anything.

Until they reached the next to last room.

The curtains to this room were drawn. Ed knocked on the door, and Daphne listened for any noise from inside.

There was none.

Ed tried the knob, and the door opened a few inches. Flies flew out of the room, followed by a waft of decayed flesh. He shut the door and waited for the deader inside to make its presence known. It never did.

"Should we check it out?" he asked.

"I need to know if there's any danger here."

Daphne raised her Mossberg in the high-ready position and

stood in front of the door. Ed turned the knob and pushed the door open. Daphne took one step inside.

Nothing stirred or attacked. The waning daylight from the open door only reached a few feet into the room, leaving most of it in darkness.

"Is anyone here?"

No response.

Ed reached in and felt around the wall until he found the light switch. He flipped it up, but the lights remained off.

"The power must be out." He grabbed the end of the curtain and pulled it back across the window, allowing light in.

"Jesus," Daphne gasped.

A corpse lay on the second bed, its legs and wrists tightly bound with rope, a pillow over its head. Its hands showed the initial stages of decay, and its clothes were clean except for a bloody tear on the lower left arm with the fatal bite wound underneath. A tire iron, one end covered in blood and gore, sat on the first bed.

Daphne approached and used the shotgun barrel to push the pillow aside, ready to fire if the thing attacked.

A swarm of flies took off from its head, filling the room. The corpse's skull had been bashed in, the upper jaw, eye sockets, and forehead pounded into a gory pile of congealed blood and bone fragments. Hundreds of maggots squirmed through the dead flesh.

Daphne ignored the body and continued to the bathroom, checking the tub for any other surprises. The area was clear. She rejoined Ed, who stood over the body saying a silent prayer. When finished, he glanced over at Daphne.

"The poor guy must have been bitten, and whoever he was with tied him up and put him out of his misery."

"That explains why there's no car in the lot," said Daphne. "They must have left him behind."

Ed placed his AK-47 against the wall, removed the blanket from the first bed, and used it to cover the body, a final act of dignity for an uncivilized death. They left the room, closing and locking the door behind them, then continued checking out their side of the motel.

HAVING COMPLETED THEIR sweep, Paul told Akiko to wait by the vending machines and walked over to the Pilot. Lisa lowered the window.

"Is everything clear?"

"On our side." Paul motioned with his head toward the front. "Akiko and I will check the office and see if we can find keys."

"Don't the doors have electronic locks?"

"Thankfully, this place is as old as shit. They still use keys, otherwise we'd be screwed because the power is off. If Daphne and Ed show up, let them know where we are."

"Okay."

Paul led the way to the front. A red Toyota Prius was parked in the drop-off zone. He moved around to the driver's side and tried the door. It was unlocked. He opened it a few inches and checked the interior. Once certain nothing dangerous lurked inside, he pulled the door open and searched around, spotting nothing of value.

Akiko tapped on the window. "Pop the trunk."

Paul searched for the latch, finding it and pulling. The trunk clicked. As Akiko rummaged through the back, Paul opened the glove compartment. It was packed with junk. He emptied it one handful at a time but found nothing useful. Just a pile of napkins, straws, and plastic utensils. Three years of old registration and inspection certificates. A pack of Trojans. A pair of gloves. And a pack of opened chewing gum hard as a rock. He left it all on the seat and did not bother closing the compartment.

"Anything useful?" he asked as he exited the car.

"It's all junk." Akiko tossed a handful of clothes back in.

"The guy must live out of his trunk. It's filled with clothes and shoes. The only thing of any use is a can of Fix-A-Flat."

"Take it with us. We might need it." Paul used the Mossberg to gesture toward the front door. "Let's see what's inside."

The automatic doors did not open due to lack of electricity. Akiko used her hands to pull both the inner and outer doors aside. Paul entered the lobby, his shotgun in the high-ready position, scanning the barrel from side to side as he approached the reception desk. The closer he got, the greater the stench of decayed flesh. Paul stopped at the opening leading behind the counter.

"Is anyone here?"

No one answered.

Paul stepped behind the front desk. The keys for the rooms hung on a rack mounted on the rear wall. He sorted through the ones for the second floor.

"There are plenty of keys for the first floor."

"I'd rather be on the second level. It gives us the advantage in case...." Paul did not want to explain.

"Good idea."

Paul eventually found three rooms together–211, 213, and 215. He removed the keyrings and slid them into his pocket, then turned to the closed door of the inner office. The stench came from there.

"Cover me."

Akiko stood on the other side of the counter, her AK-47 ready to fire. Paul moved over to the door and gently knocked. When he received no response, he turned the knob and pushed it aside.

The body of an Indian man sat in a chair positioned vertically to the desk. His head rested on the top of the backrest and his arms hung by the sides. The guy had used a steak knife from the kitchen to slice open both arms, from the wrists up to the elbows, making sure to sever the arteries so he would bleed out quickly. Two large pools of dried blood formed on either side of the chair, merging around the base wheels. Because he was sealed in the office, insects had not begun to feed off the carcass. The knife sat on the desk, along with the keys to the car and a cell phone.

"Was he bitten?" asked Akiko.

"It doesn't look like it. I think he just gave up and took his own life."

"What now?"

"We have to leave him here." Paul stepped in, took the keys, and scanned the room for anything of value, but saw nothing. He stepped out and shut the door behind him.

"I want to make sure no deaders are hiding in this area, then I want to check out the kitchen for supplies."

THE HORDE OF deaders that had attacked Paul's group in Raphine had continued following the two vehicles. However, after running for a mile, they forgot what they had been chasing and slowed until the mass of living dead shambled along Raphine Road.

Eventually, they came to the intersection with Brownsburg Turnpike. Without a straight path to continue on, the deaders clogged the area. A few staggered north or south along the road. Some crossed over into the tree line and continued into the woods.

A deader in priest's garb, the skin and muscles on its left arm chewed away below the elbow, stood in the center of the intersection, confused about what to do or where to go. Then it detected a scent. Food? No, it did not have that aroma of fresh meat, but it smelled of something familiar. Turning left, the priest deader stumbled down the road, following the scent.

It found the source a minute later—one of its own, recently mangled, lying along the side of the road. Whatever mishap that befell it churned up the stench of rotting flesh and congealed blood. The priest deader had picked up that odor many times since its turning. All it knew was that the smell did not come from food, so it had no meaning.

The priest deader continued walking south along Brownsburg Turnpike, the same direction in which Paul's group had traveled.

One by one, the rest of the horde fell in behind the priest deader.

Chapter Twelve

I T TOOK LESS than an hour for Paul's group to set up their defenses for the night, if you can call the makeshift barricade a defense. They had removed one of the two beds from Rooms 211 and 215 and used them to block either end of the outside corridor. The remainder of the furniture from all three rooms was then piled on top, creating a blockade. It would not hold against a horde but would slow the living dead down long enough for them to escape. Paul parked the Pilot by the stairs at the front of the motel but in the opposite lot, and Ed parked the RAM by the rear stairs to ensure that, in a worst-case scenario, the group would have at least one means of escape.

Akiko, Lisa, the kids, and Gojira took the center room since it still had two beds. Ed took Room 211, and Paul and Daphne took Room 215. Once the barricades had been put in place and everyone had eaten, the group took advantage of the safe surroundings to get some much-needed rest. The watches were two hours each, beginning with Lisa and followed by Daphne, Akiko, Ed, and Paul.

AKIKO NAPPED ON the bed, resting before her watch began in four hours. Lisa sat on the second bed, propped up against the headboard, watching the kids sitting on the floor playing with Gojira. She was so proud of her daughter and Toshii for being understanding of Tommy's social anxiety and doing what they could to make him feel comfortable. Even Gojira spent time with the boy, playing and nuzzling with him. It was shitty enough to lose your parents and then your friends. Being rescued by people who treated you like an outcast would have been a nightmare. Thankfully, Tommy fit in with them, so he wouldn't feel isolated during the apocalypse.

Judith stood, crossed the room, and sat on the bed beside her mother. Lisa wrapped her arms around the girl and pulled her in for a hug.

"Mom, will we make it through all this alive?"

"Of course, sweety."

"Don't lie to me," Judith whispered.

"I'm not."

"I know when you're lying to me. You have the same tone in your voice now as you did when you told me Santa and the Easter Bunny were real."

"I thought you believed in them."

Judith shook her head.

"Then why did you tell me you did?"

"I didn't want to hurt your feelings. Now it's your turn. Tell me the truth. Are we going to make it through this alive?"

Lisa smiled. It's amazing how quickly children grow up when they have to.

"To be honest, I'd say our chances are fifty-fifty."

"And that's because we have Paul and Daphne helping us."

"We wouldn't be alive without them."

"I know." Judith stared at the floor. "I hope they don't get killed keeping us alive."

"Me, too." Lisa struggled to think of the proper thing to say that was supportive yet honest. "Some of us will survive this, some of us won't."

"Like Grandma?"

Lisa's memory of killing her infirm mother to prevent the woman from being eaten or turned overwhelmed her. She choked back her emotions and desperately tried to maintain a cheerful façade for Judith.

"Yes, like Grandma."

"I don't want to lose you, too."

"You won't."

"We thought the same thing about Becca and Ian."

Damn, she was growing up too quick. Lisa hugged her daughter so Judith would not see the tears streaming down her cheeks. "I'll do everything possible to keep us both alive. And God forbid, if something happens to me, Paul and Daphne will take as good care of you as I would. Always know that I love you more than anything. And I'll always be here for you."

"Even as an angel?"

"Yes."

Judith hugged her mother tightly. Lisa kissed her on the top of her head.

"You go back with the boys. I have to start my watch."

"Okay. Mom." Judith stood. "Be careful out there."

"I will."

Lisa took her AK-47 and left the room. She had barely closed the door when she broke down, leaning against the railing and sobbing uncontrollably.

DAPHNE WAS MORE than three-quarters of the way through her watch. She leaned forward onto the railing overlooking the parking lot. She had long since leaned her gun against one of the barricades only a few feet from her, knowing it was doubtful she would need it. The only activity around the motel came from wildlife that sauntered onto the grounds. Three raccoons emerged from the woods to ransack the motel dumpster, abandoning their bonanza only when a stray dog scared them off. Ten minutes ago, a family of deer came down the road, turned into the parking lot, and cautiously made their way to the opposite end, only to disappear into the trees. It gave her a sense of comfort. If deaders were nearby, the wildlife would have long since vacated the area.

Once the stray dog gave up his foraging and headed home, dark thoughts began to push back into Daphne's mind. How long would this nightmare last, assuming there would be an end to it? Their group had already experienced more horror in the past week than most people would in a lifetime. And they had not suffered the worst of it. Their losses had been regrettable but minor compared to what they could have been. They had barely survived their encounters with the hordes in Leesburg and Front Royal, and those were small cities. The only reason she and Paul had survived Pittsburg was because they were on the outskirts of the city when the outbreak began and, even then, barely made it out alive.

Daphne's mind could barely comprehend the nightmare that must be taking place in large cities like New York, Chicago, Dallas-Fort Worth, and Los Angeles. She imagined hordes of the living dead, several million strong, rampaging up and down the coasts. Or even worse, heading inland once the food ran out. No one could survive that. The Rocky Mountains would stop or, at least, slow down those deaders from the west. The Mississippi River would be a major deterrent for those coming from the east. Everyone in their path would be slaughtered.

She remembered the images from the tsunamis that flooded Japan back in 2011. One video that always stood out in her mind was a lone truck racing for safety down a coastal road as the water flowed in and washed it away. The same thing was happening now, only this time it was a tidal wave of the living dead flowing across the country, devouring everything in its path.

A brief vision flashed through Daphne's mind of sitting in the passenger seat of the SUV and watching a wall of deaders racing toward them. A shiver ran down her spine. She involuntarily looked to her right to make certain the Mossberg still leaned against the barricade.

Maybe going north was a bad idea. They would have to drive over fifteen hundred miles before reaching safety. The smartest move might be heading west and crossing the Mississippi into the safe zone between the river and the Rockies.

Daphne chastised herself for letting fear get the better of her. The chances of the hordes making it that far inland so quickly seemed small, especially compared to the risk of trying to find a way across the Mississippi. As Tommy had pointed out, most crossings were in major cities where they could never fight their way through the deaders. Any bridges outside populated areas were more than likely either destroyed to prevent deaders from getting across or were impassable because thousands of others had the same idea and became trapped.

Their best bet was to keep to the current plan and head north as quickly as possible. And to do that, she had to keep her head in the game.

The opening of a door Daphne caught her attention. Akiko emerged from her room, quietly closed the door behind her, and joined Daphne.

"I assume everything is quiet."

"Nothing but wildlife."

"Good."

"How are the kids?" Daphne asked.

"They're asleep. With no TV or electronics, there's nothing else for them to do."

"How are they holding up?"

"They're doing good considering what we're going through. Having Tommy join the group has helped keep them distracted." Akiko paused. "I could ask the same of you."

"I've been too busy to concentrate much on Tommy."

"No. I mean, how are you holding up?"

"Good."

"You're good at killing the living dead but terrible at lying."

Daphne chuckled. "Is it that obvious?"

"Yes. We rely on you, Paul, and Ed. The rest of us are not cut out for this."

"You handled yourself well on Skyline Drive."

"I must learn if I'm going to keep the kids alive. If someone had told me a month ago that I'd be killing deaders, I would have taken away their *sake*."

"Tell me about it. I worked in an office before all this. The worst I ever dealt with was irate customers on the phone. I was trapped inside my car, too scared to move, when Paul found me. Thank God he took pity on my sorry ass, or I'd be one of those things."

"You fight very well."

"You do what you have to if you want to survive."

"Sometimes survival is beyond our control. My great-grandparents lived in Hiroshima during World War II. My great-grandmother left the city to care for her dying aunt and was not there when the Americans dropped the bomb. My great-grandfather did not survive."

"But your great-grandmother did?"

Akiko shook her head. "Her aunt lived in Nagasaki."

"Sorry."

"It is what it is. We lived in Tokyo. Toshii and I would not be alive if my husband had not decided to take us on vacation to the States. He worked seventy hours a week and wanted us to have quality time as a family. It was our first vacation as a family since Toshii was born. His decision kept us out of one of the worst spots for the outbreak, but it cost him his life."

Daphne had no idea how to respond.

"Have you and Paul spent the night together?" asked Akiko.

"We haven't been apart since the shit hit the fan."

"That's not what I meant."

"I know. And no, we haven't."

"If you like each other, you should."

"It's the middle of the apocalypse."

"All the more reason." Akiko placed her hand on Daphne's. "Look what we've been through already. We're not all going to make it out of this alive."

"That's morbid."

"But it's the truth. Live your life to the fullest while you still have time. If something happens to Paul, you'll always regret the time you didn't have together. Believe me, I know." Akiko placed her AK-47 against the barricade and handed Daphne the shotgun. "Your watch is over. Get some rest."

"Thank you." Daphne hugged Akiko and headed for her room.

Paul was asleep under the covers of the bed. He snored lightly. Daphne stripped naked, went over to the bed, and shook him awake.

"Move over so I can have some room."

Paul stared at her, groggy and confused. Daphne lifted the covers and slid up against Paul.

"It's safer to sleep with your clothes on," he said.

"I'm not interested in sleeping."

ED SPENT MOST of his watch concentrating on a black bear that had strolled out of the woods and made its way to the dumpster. It crawled inside and scavenged around, looking for any food not already taken by the raccoons.

He wondered if, like himself, the bear had lost its mate to the deader outbreak. So far, they had not seen any of the living dead gorging on animals, but it made sense. Humans had been mostly eliminated, and those who had survived were either hiding or making their way to some hoped-for safe zone. With their food supply diminished, the living dead would have to choose between starving or finding an alternate food source.

Usually, wildlife flourished after catastrophes like Chernobyl and Fukushima. However, if they become sources of food, many species might become extinct, just like man.

Like man.

Deer and livestock would suffer the most. Smaller, quicker animals would have the best chance of surviving. However, it would be fascinating to watch a grizzly or a pack of coyotes battling the living dead. He wondered if a bitten animal would turn into a deader, then quickly pushed that thought away. The last thing he wanted to envision was fighting off a deader bear or a nest of living dead rats.

Ed sighed. Even if wildlife became the next food source, at least the poor animals would not have to live in constant fear with the knowledge that the world as they knew it had ended. Would they miss a devoured mate or cub the way he missed Becca?

The thought depressed him. They had been so occupied since encountering the living dead on the Delaware Bay Bridge that he did not have much time to think of her. She might be alive today if it wasn't for Sparky. That asshole got what he deserved, though Ed wished it had been him who pushed Sparky off the bridge tower rather than Paul. At least justice had been served.

Ed almost gave up that night. Life without Becca was even more hellish than the nightmare they were currently going through. The group needed all the help they could get if they ever hoped to get the children to safety, which seemed futile. Even if a handful of humans survived this, what life would they have? They would inherit a world inhabited by the dead. Even if, somehow, they took back the globe, then what? Life would revert to colonial times, or even worse, a medieval society. Few people would be able to keep up that lifestyle. Maybe it would be better if we all died out now.

Maybe this was God's plan. Kill off the world's population, only this time with a sea of the living dead rather than a Biblical flood.

The bear scrounging through the dumpster climbed to the outer rim and peered out. It issued a grunt that Ed could have sworn sounded like fear. The animal scrambled over the rim so quickly it tipped over the dumpster. It roared again and raced off into the woods behind the motel, taking one final glance over its shoulder.

Ed heard what had frightened the bear. Moaning and snarling.

Looking to his right, Ed saw a horde of deaders rushing across the motel parking lot in pursuit of the bear. Most disappeared into the woods.

Several dozen ran over to the overturned dumpster, the first ones pushing their way in. A frenzy erupted between those that had entered and the ones stuck outside. A few seconds later, the first deaders emerged, chewing on the rotten limbs of a human. Others shoved past, coming out with more severed limbs. A female child deader no more than ten years old crawled out, dragging the victim's intestines. It knelt in the middle of the parking lot and began feasting on the severed end, congealed blood and feces dripping between its lips. Those deaders that had not yet gotten inside converged on the trail of intestines, ripping it into pieces and gorging on it.

The final deader, a priest with most of its left arm eaten away, made its way into the dumpster and came out with a head clutched in its decayed hands. It bit down on the left eye and yanked the orb out of its socket. The optic nerves stopped the thing from eating. It opened its mouth, bit down on the nerves, tore loose the eyeball, and chewed.

A dozen more meandered around the parking lot. Three raised their heads and sniffed the air, picking up fresh food's scent nearby.

Ed slowly moved back from the railing, opened the door to Paul's and Daphne's room, and stepped inside.

"Don't make a sound," he whispered. "We have a horde of deaders outside."

Chapter Thirteen

PAUL JUMPED OUT of bed naked and quickly put on his clothes. "How many?"

"About fifty in the lot. Another few hundred chased a bear into the woods."

"Fuck." Daphne also dressed rapidly.

"Did they see you?" asked Paul.

Ed shook his head. "I'm going to warn the others."

"Tell them to stay in their room until they hear from me."

Ed nodded and cautiously left.

"What do we do now?" asked Daphne.

Paul buckled his pants and slid on his socks and boots. "Pray they don't find us."

ED HUGGED THE wall until he reached Room 213. Fortunately, the girls had not locked the door. He slid inside.

Lisa woke with a start. "What's go—"

"Shh." Ed moved to the center of the room. "There's a horde of deaders outside."

"Dear God."

Lisa woke up Akiko and warned her about the danger, then they roused the kids to tell them. When everyone was up, Lisa stepped over to Ed.

"What are we going to do?"

"I don't know. Paul and Daphne are assessing the situation."

"Hopefully, they'll move on," said Akiko.

Tommy shook his head. "We know that's not going to happen."

PAUL WAITED FOR Daphne to finish dressing, and the two quietly exited their room. She pulled the door against the jamb but did not close it, afraid the click might attract attention. They stayed against the wall and stared out over the lot.

Placing a hand on Paul's shoulder, as much for comfort as to get his attention, Daphne leaned close and whispered, "Where did they come from?"

"They probably followed us from Raphine."

"How are we going to get out of this?"

Paul slowly stepped over to the railing and leaned over to examine the parking lot. After a minute, he moved back and joined Daphne.

"Our only option is to sneak downstairs to the cars and get out of here."

"We have the high ground. Why don't we pick them off?"

"We might take these out, but if what Ed said is true, several hundred more are near here. Gunfire will bring those down on us, then we're screwed."

Daphne pointed to the twin barricades. "How do you intend to break them down without making noise?"

"Shit. I hadn't thought of that." Paul ran his right hand through his hair as he contemplated their next move. "We'll have to do it as quietly as possible. I'll tell the others what we have planned. You stay here and keep an eye on them."

As Paul went to warn the others, Daphne watched the deaders roam through the lot. The sight of so many between them and their vehicles unnerved her. So far, the group always had a chance to fight their way out, however slim it might be. This time, they were trapped. Daphne suppressed a gut feeling that they might not survive this time.

The door to Room 213 opened and the others silently emerged. The kids stayed against the wall, with Toshii holding Gojira's mouth closed and Judith comforting the dog, who thankfully remained quiet. Both kids were terrified but hid it well. Tommy remained stoic.

The adults moved to the barricade facing the rear of the building and carefully removed one piece of furniture at a time, lifting and cautiously placing them on the walkway so as not to make any noise. Every few seconds, Daphne would glance over the railing to make sure none of the deaders had detected them.

So far, so good.

Paul and Ed were moving a table off the bed when one of its legs became entangled with the leg of a chair. When they raised the table, they inadvertently yanked the chair, knocking it over the railing. Lisa and Akiko reached out to catch it, the latter grabbing the backrest. The chair banged against the railing, slipped from Akiko's hand, and tumbled into the parking lot.

Every deader spun around, searching for the source of the noise.

Paul rushed down to the barricade facing the front of the motel, grabbed a table from the top, and tossed it over the railing. The corner fell onto a deader in a business suit, crushing its skull. The commotion drew the attention of the rest of the living dead to that spot. Paul aimed his Vepr into the horde and fired, taking down the first two with headshots.

"Come on, you decayed fucks! Fresh food on the second floor!"

"What the hell are you doing?" asked Daphne, terror in her eyes.

"Buying you and the others time to get out of here."

"They'll kill you," cried Akiko.

"The barricade will hold them long enough for the rest of you to get to the cars. I'll join you in a minute."

Proving his point, every deader in the parking lot rushed for the forward stairwell. The frenzied snarls and stomping of feet could already be heard coming up the steps.

Paul removed the Pilot's keys from his pocket and tossed them to Daphne. "Go while you have a chance."

A deader in a jogging outfit, its shoulders and upper chest shredded to the bones, raced around the corner and attacked the barricade. Paul raised the Vepr and fired, blasting away the back of its head and throwing the body into the deader behind it.

The sound of several hundred rampaging deaders came from the woods behind the motel.

AKIKO USHERED THE kids over what little remained of the barricade by Room 215 and toward the rear stairs. Lisa led the way, her AK-47 raised and ready to fire on anything that came after them.

Ed grabbed Daphne by the arm and pulled her away.

She hesitated. "I'm staying with Paul."

"The kids need you more."

"Fuck," Daphne mumbled under her breath and followed Ed.

PAUL CONTINUED PUMPING rounds into the pack of deaders. Each shot launched a swarm of flies and wasps, many hovering around Paul's face. He ignored the twin stings to his forehead and the one on his neck, continuing to pump round after round into the horde frantic to reach him.

When empty, he reloaded the shotgun, which gave the living dead a chance to climb over the bodies of those already killed and tear away at the barricade. One deader in a blood-soaked EMT uniform, using a chair for support, climbed the pile until it stood above Paul. The chair broke loose, plunging the deader over the railing. It landed headfirst onto the asphalt below. Three more attempted to surge through the opening. Paul took them down with headshots, the bodies collapsing on the barricade and blocking the gap.

As Paul fired on the dead, he listened for the start of the vehicles' engines, which would be his cue to join the others.

LISA WAS HALFWAY down the stairs. She paused on the landing and raised her hands for the others to stop. They did. Toshii wrapped his hands around Gojira's jaws.

A horde of deaders poured out of the woods into the parking lot. Because it was still dark, none of them spotted the group, their attention drawn to the melee up front and the pack fighting their way up the front stairwell.

Lisa waited until the last one had passed before waving the others on. Once on ground level, she stood five feet in front of the last step, ready to provide cover if necessary.

Ed rushed ahead and opened the doors to the RAM. Akiko quietly helped the kids and Gojira into the back. Ed went around the pick-up, holding the handles in the open position, gently shutting the doors, then releasing the handle so they locked into place. Both adults jumped in front, Ed taking the driver's seat.

Daphne leaned in and whispered.

"Ed, give me sixty seconds before you start her up. Stay as long as you can, but haul ass once the deaders come after you."

"What about Paul?"

"You worry about keeping them safe." She motioned toward the kids seated in back. "We'll stick around and wait for Paul."

Ed nodded his understanding.

Daphne made her way to the southern end of the building and peered around the corner. No deaders were on this side. Snapping her fingers, she caught Lisa's attention and signaled for her to follow. The two women ran down to the Pilot. Daphne slid into the driver's seat while Lisa rode shotgun.

Gunfire echoed from the motel's other side, meaning Paul was still alive.

PAUL LOST TRACK of how many deaders he had taken down. Not that the number mattered since several hundred were still trying to get to him. The growing pile of bodies in front of the barricade made it easier for the horde to gain leverage. Even worse, the weight of the pack put too much stress on the barricade, which was in danger of caving in. He had a minute left at most before it collapsed, exposing him to the horde.

"Come on, Daphne."

"READY?" ASKED DAPHNE.

Lisa shook her head. "No. But go ahead."

Daphne slid the keys into the ignition and turned.

The Pilot's engine turned over.

ED COULD BARELY hear anything over the turmoil generated by the horde. He thought he detected the sound of the Pilot starting but could not be sure.

"How long has it been?" he asked.

Akiko glanced at her watch. "Fifty seconds."

"Close enough."

Ed shut the door and turned the ignition. The engine stuttered but would not turn over. He tried it a second time, applying pressure on the accelerator. The engine roared to life. Ed pressed his foot on the pedal to make certain it didn't stall.

From the back seat, Tommy calmly warned, "We have company."

Glancing into the rearview mirror, Ed saw a pack of the

living dead rounding the rear end of the motel.

BECAUSE OF THE noise being made by the battle around the barricade, only a few of the living dead on the fringes detected the Pilot starting up. A dozen or so stumbled into the parking lot, searching in vain for their meal.

One deader, a burly guy with a long beard and wearing a black t-shirt and a Harley Davidson leather vest, a chunk of flesh bitten out of its left arm, staggered through the alley between the rooms and front office, heading toward the parking lot on the southern side.

Those at the rear end of the lot heard the RAM in its first attempt to start. One deader, an obese naked guy with its throat torn out, turned and scanned the area. When the pick-up's engine started on the second try, it pinpointed the source and bolted for the end of the motel. Over forty deaders followed.

When the pack rounded the corner and spotted the RAM, they attacked.

ED SLAMMED HIS foot onto the gas pedal. The RAM shot around the motel into the southern lot. Most of the pack followed the pick-up. More than a dozen broke off and rushed the Pilot.

Eight deaders at the rear of the pack heard gunfire on the second floor. They veered left and rushed up the rear stairwell, heading for the noise they associated with food.

WHEN PAUL HEARD the RAM and Pilot start, he breathed a sigh of relief. The barricade leaned precariously and would collapse any second. He fired several more rounds into those deaders at the top of the pile of furniture, shouldered his bag of spare ammo, then spun around and headed for the rear stairwell.

Eight of the living dead rounded the corner. On spotting him, they lunged. Paul raised his Vepr and fired, taking down the first three before he ran out of ammunition. The remaining five closed in for the kill.

Behind him, the barricade collapsed.

DAPHNE WATCHED AS the pack followed Ed around the rear of the motel, more than half chasing the RAM and the rest coming after her.

"Shit," muttered Lisa.

Daphne turned forward in time to see the biker deader emerge from the alley. On seeing the Pilot, it screamed and charged. A second later, another thirty or so deaders raced out of the alley. With only a moment to respond, Daphne shifted into drive and raced across the parking lot, swerving around the front of the building and heading back into the northern lot.

"What are you doing?" asked Lisa.

"Looking for Paul."

SEEING THEY WERE about to be overwhelmed, Ed pulled away and headed for the exit.

"Stay with Daphne," said Akiko.

"What about the kids?"

"It doesn't matter. We can't afford to lose them."

Ed spun the steering wheel to the left and followed Daphne.

PAUL HAD ONLY one option open, as bad as it was.

Crawling up onto the railing, he steadied himself as best he could and jumped, grabbing the edge of the flat roof. The stones dug into his fingers, but the pain was better than being eaten alive. He pulled himself up as far as possible before swinging his left leg up and over the edge.

A lanky deader still wearing eyeglasses covered in blood lunged at him. Using all his strength, Paul rolled onto the roof. The bag of ammo dug into his side, sending a bolt of pain down his left leg and across his back. The deader tumbled over the railing into the horde beneath, missing its prey by inches.

Paul lay there for a moment, exhausted, catching his breath and trying to figure out how to get out of this mess.

He heard the Pilot and RAM rushing through the parking lot beneath him. Jumping to his feet, he watched the two vehicles race down the lot and circle around behind the motel. He ran to the other side of the roof, jumping and waving his hands.

"UP THERE." LISA pointed to the roof.

Paul stood on the edge, desperately trying to get their attention.

Daphne slowed and rolled down her window halfway. "We'll lead the deaders away and come back for you."

Paul shook his head. "Go somewhere safe. I'll figure a way out of here."

Pretending not to hear him, Daphne rolled up the window and headed for the exit. Ed stayed ten feet behind her. Once on the street, she turned left back toward Raphine.

Most of the horde followed.

Close to fifty of the living dead stayed behind, desperate to get at the food on the roof.

Chapter Fourteen

L ISA SAT SIDEWAYS in the seat, watching the deaders. They could have easily outrun them, but Daphne drove only fast enough to stay a hundred feet ahead of them. Lisa shifted to face forward.

"Where are we heading?"

"We need to find a side road that returns to this one." Daphne handed her a map. "And we need to find it before we get back to Raphine."

T HE MAJORITY OF the horde chased the two vehicles north along Maury Road. Paul knew Daphne and Ed would be back, though shaking off the deaders might take a while. He needed the time to clear away the deaders that had stayed behind.

The question was, how many had stayed behind?

Paul reloaded the Vepr, slid the ammo bag over his shoulder, and moved to the edge of the roof overlooking the northern parking lot. The first rays of sunlight crested the horizon, providing enough light to see his surroundings.

As for a way off the roof, he saw none. All the stairwells ended on the second floor, none coming up to the roof, and no skylights or hatches led below. Which meant his only way down would be the same as he came up—over the side of the roof. That option did not appeal to him because he almost did not make it up.

Paul heard deaders shambling along the exterior corridor

but could not determine how many were there. Eight remained in the lot, five staggering around aimlessly. Over a dozen lay in a pile below the railing, including the one that lunged at him and toppled over the side and the two it had landed on. Their spines must have been broken since their heads moved, but not their bodies.

"Hey, meat sacks!"

The deaders on the exterior corridor beneath him and those in the lot, including the three immobile ones, worked themselves into a frenzy. One deader, with its entire left arm and left torso eaten away, spotted Paul, snarled, and raced for the stairs to the second floor. The others followed. Another deader leaned back against the railing and peered up, spotting Paul. It snapped its teeth. Paul aimed the shotgun over the side and pulled the trigger, vaporizing its head.

He waited for others of the living dead to stick out their heads, but none did. Scanning the roof, he noticed it ran in a straight line from one end of the motel to the other, with no outcrops he could use to shoot from. It would make his job that much harder. As the old saying goes, if the mountains wouldn't come to Muhammad, Muhammad would have to go to the mountains.

Laying prone, Paul inched his way to the edge of the roof and peered over. Nearly thirty of the living dead gathered in front of the rooms. Getting an accurate aim would be impossible from this position.

Holding the shotgun's barrel in his right hand, and keeping it close to his chest, Paul grasped the trigger guard in his left and extended his arm as far out as possible. He attempted to aim at a deader in a bloody, tattered nightgown and pulled the trigger. The round struck just above the sternum, shattering the ribcage and heart, and blasting the spine in half. The nightgown deader's head fell backward, still snarling as its immobile body collapsed onto the floor.

Attracted by the noise, the remaining deaders lunged at

Paul's exposed upper body. He rolled back onto the roof before they could reach him. Paul crawled back to the edge but did not expose himself this time. He placed the shotgun's barrel against the lower rim of the roof, used his left hand to press down on the stock to hold the weapon in place, and with the right left, repeatedly squeezed the trigger until the Vepr ran out of rounds. Buckshot tore into decayed flesh, and bodies collapsed. Congealed blood, gore, and a mass of agitated flies and wasps flew out over the parking lot.

Getting up, Paul moved down the roof twenty feet and peered over the side again. He had taken down three deaders and blasted holes in five more that did nothing to slow them down.

This was going to take a lot longer than he had anticipated.

"TAKE THIS LEFT," said Lisa. "The one right after the bend in the river."

"Are you sure?"

"It'll take us to a series of back roads that'll eventually bring us back onto the turnpike."

Daphne swung the Pilot onto the road and accelerated to put more distance between herself and the horde and to give Ed room to maneuver.

THE SUDDEN MANEUVER caught Ed off guard. He turned at the last second, the rear wheels squealing in protest. The right tires dug into the soft sand along the shoulder, slowing down the RAM. For a second, Ed feared they might get stuck. Applying more gas, the pick-up lurched forward and back onto the road, quickly catching up with Daphne.

Judith shifted in her seat and looked out the rear window. "They're still behind us."

"That's okay," comforted Akiko. "We want them to follow

us until we have a chance to lose them."

"Are you sure?"

"Yes. Trust me." Akiko turned to face front and whispered to Ed, "I hope Daphne knows what she's doing."

"She does," answered Ed. He didn't vocalize his concern that being on back roads might lead to something up ahead they could not get past.

PAUL HAD BEEN battling the deaders for more than fifteen minutes, occasionally luring one to stick out its head so he could shoot it easily, but mostly leaning over the edge of the roof and awkwardly firing. The more he culled out the pack, the more difficult it became to hit the remaining targets. He had used up twice as much ammunition as in the beginning with half the results. Assuming all the deaders were on the exterior corridor below him, there were about fifteen left to kill off.

DAPHNE SWITCHED HER attention between the road ahead and checking the mirrors. "I'm going to take the next turn and lead them away."

"No," responded Lisa. "Most of these are dead ends."

"Shit."

The damn deaders maintained their pace, showing no signs of tiring. Daphne accelerated a few miles per hour.

Lisa studied the map, suddenly becoming excited. "Take the next right onto Back Draft Road. It's only a few hundred feet ahead. There are plenty of roads off it where we can lose them."

Daphne sped up to put some distance between them and the living dead, then switched on her right directional so Ed wouldn't be caught off guard this time.

"Turn here," warned Lisa.

Both vehicles veered onto Back Draft Road, the horde remaining close behind.

ROLLING AWAY FROM the end of the roof, Paul groaned. The constant leaning over the side and jumping back before the deaders got him, combined with the rough, gravelly surface, had started to take a toll. His back, shoulders, and elbows ached, slowing his reaction time. And all the activity only aggravated his bruised left leg. At this rate, one of the living dead would get him before he could duck away.

Reloading the Vepr, Paul stood, grabbed the bag of ammunition, and moved down to the far end of the roof. Laying prone, he peered over the side.

Nine of the living dead stood beneath where he had been moments before, tripping over the corpses piled up around them. He had cleaned out more than he thought. Leaning forward, Paul aimed and fired three rounds in succession, blowing apart the heads of two deaders and blasting the right arm off a third.

The others charged.

Paul began to roll back when one deader in Air Force BDU jumped up and clutched Paul's left forearm. Most of Paul's body was on the roof, otherwise the weight would have dragged him into the pack. The Air Force deader hung on, trying to lift itself to bite him, its teeth snapping inches from Paul's arm. It did not have the strength to reach Paul, but neither did Paul have the strength to pull away. The others surrounded the Air Force deader, frantically reaching for Paul. One tall deader in a tattered plaid shirt wrapped its hand around Paul's inner elbow, pulling him toward the edge.

Paul still clutched the Vepr in his right hand. He placed the barrel against the Air Force deader's face and pulled the trigger. The skull exploded in a spray of congealed blood and gore. It fell to the floor and released its grip, no longer threatening to pull him off the roof. Leaning over slightly and switching the angle, Paul aimed at the tall deader and fired. The round tore through its chest, punching its way out the back and lodging in the motel room window behind it. The second caught it in the left eye, blowing off the side of its face and splattering brain matter across the wall.

Paul started to roll back when a deader wearing an over-sized football jersey rushed forward, hoping to grab his left arm. Instead, it wrapped its hands around the Vepr and pulled. Rather than trusting common sense and letting go, Paul tried to maintain his grip. The deader ripped the shotgun from Paul's hands and toppled over the railing.

And yanked Paul off the roof.

He held on to the edge, his dangling legs making an entic-ing target, the living dead version of fresh meat hanging in a butcher shop. Paul kicked his legs violently, hoping none of the remaining deaders would get a grip, knowing his efforts were useless.

Paul had reached the end of the line.

At least he would take out as many of these motherfuckers as possible.

A deader dressed in a tan deputy's uniform grabbed Paul's right leg and, rather than bite, pulled it. Paul released his grip, allowing the thing to drag him into the exterior corridor. Paul's back hit the railing, the pain causing his vision to blur momen-tarily. He toppled forward, knocking the deader over. His left knee landed on the cement, sending an excruciating pain up his bruised leg. The right drove into the deader's chest, accompa-nied by the shattering of bones. Paul was grateful it was the deader's sternum and not his knee.

The other three deaders rushed him. Paul rolled to his left, sliding his knife from its sheath. He collided with the legs of a deader with its wrists handcuffed behind its back, knocking it over and into the other two coming up from behind. One deader, naked from the waist up, its abdomen ripped open, half its entrails hanging out, stumbled against the wall. The second deader, a child no more than six, fell backward onto the floor.

Paul jumped to his feet, momentarily dizzy. Seeing his chance, he went after the handcuffed deader, which struggled to its feet. Grabbing it by the back of the head with his left hand and pushing it forward, Paul used his right to shove the knife into where the neck meets the skull, jamming it up to the hilt and twisting. The handcuffed deader went limp.

Paul withdrew the blade, stood, and spun around as the topless deader lunged. It lost its balance as it attempted to step over the deputy and the handcuffed deaders. Paul rushed forward and drove the blade under its jaw and up into the brain. The milky white eyes widened, and the deader froze. Paul turned the blade at a ninety-degree angle, scrambling its brainstem. As he jumped back, the topless deader collapsed onto the deputy's upper body, knocking it back to the floor and pinning it.

By now, the child deader had risen to its feet and attacked. Paul waited until it was almost on him, then moved to the side. As it passed, he clutched the back of its collar with his left hand, slammed its head against the railing, and plunged the knife into its right ear, putting the thing out of its misery.

Going over to the deputy deader, Paul rolled the topless deader to the side and plunged his knife into the former's eye, again twisting it around until it stopped moving. Pulling out the blade, he wiped it clean on the uniform, sheathed it, and leaned against the railing to catch his breath.

Jesus, he had survived this, though he had no idea how. Paul figured by now he would have been one of the living—

Paul heard a snarl from behind him and turned as the priest deader lunged.

"TAKE THE NEXT left," ordered Lisa.

Daphne seemed confused. "If we stay straight, the road will

curve back to the turnpike."

"It's all open ground. They'll just follow us back to the motel." Lisa pointed to the left. "According to the map, that road will take us through the woods where we can lose them."

Daphne made the turn. Ed followed. The deaders continued after the two vehicles.

The road continued for several hundred feet before veering right into the woods.

"Gun it," said Lisa. "Now's our chance to ditch them."

Daphne pushed her foot down on the accelerator. The Pilot shot forward. A few seconds later, they exited the woods with open fields on each side.

"That's not going to help much."

"Just keep hauling ass." Lisa motioned ahead to where the road ended at a crossroads. "Turn right, then put some distance between us, or this won't work."

"THANK GOD WE'RE finally leaving those things behind," said Akiko.

"How much distance did we put between us?" asked Ed.

Toshii turned around and glanced out back. "Only a few hundred feet."

AT THE END of the road, Daphne swung right. The back end fishtailed slightly, but she quickly regained control and sped up. The two vehicles entered a stretch of road with trees on either side.

"About a mile up ahead is Route 731. Take a right onto it."

Daphne brought the Pilot's speed up to over sixty miles per hour. As they left the woods, they approached a small road on their right.

"Is that it?" asked Daphne.

"The next one." Lisa looked behind her. She didn't see any

deaders chasing them.

Daphne turned right, heading back into the woods.

"The road makes a sharp left, then an immediate right. Shortly after that, it'll break off into three directions. You want to take the road on the left. The other two are dead ends."

Daphne followed Lisa's directions, driving as fast as possible without wrecking the SUV. A few minutes later, they exited the woods. Half a mile up ahead, Route 731 ended at another crossroads.

Lisa folded the map and placed it beside her. "Turn right up ahead and follow that road until it takes us back to Browns-burg Turnpike."

Daphne grew nervous. Everything around here for miles was open farmland. Once she made the right turn, she gunned it, hoping to reach the turnpike before the deaders emerged from the woods and spotted them.

As ED WATCHED Daphne make the turn, he realized where they were. They might make it as long as none of the deaders followed them.

"Kids, keep your eyes on the woods behind us, and let me know if you spot any deaders."

"Sure thing," said Tommy.

All three shifted in their seats and watched the tree line. Gojira joined in, though he had no idea what they were doing.

Several minutes passed. The two vehicles raced back to the turnpike, disappearing behind a copse of trees.

"Did you see anything?" asked Akiko.

Judith shook her head.

Akiko glanced over at Ed. "I think we did it."

Ed felt relieved.

A minute later, Daphne pulled into the parking lot of the Brownsburg Post Office and waved for Ed to pull up beside her. Ed did so and rolled down the passenger window.

"Did we lose them?" she asked.

"I think so. We haven't seen any deaders since we last left the woods."

"Good." Daphne grew anxious. "Follow me. We have to save Paul."

Chapter Fifteen

DAPHNE PULLED INTO the hotel parking lot and slowed, scanning the area. Decayed bodies lay strewn everywhere. A mound of a dozen or more piled up at the base of the exterior corridor beneath the first barricade. A mass of the dead lay in front of the barricade, with a handful scattered around the other. Pools of congealed blood and limbs formed on the ground or dripped from the second-floor walkway. Except for swarms of insects feeding off the dead, and a deader in priest's garb, the skin and muscles on its left arm chewed away below the elbow, staggering around on a broken ankle, nothing moved.

There was no sign of Paul.

Daphne shifted into PARK, stepped out of the Pilot, and took down the priest deader with a single round to the head. Once it collapsed onto the asphalt, she turned toward the motel.

"Paul?"

Lisa came up and clasped her hand. "Is that a good idea?"

Daphne ignored her. "Paul, where are you?"

No response, not even the snarling of the living dead.

Daphne made her way to the stairwell leading to the second floor.

Lisa tried to stop her. "It's too dangerous."

"I have to find Paul," Daphne snapped.

Ed pulled up alongside Lisa and rolled down his window. "What's going on?"

"Daphne can't find Paul."

"Shit," he said under his breath.

"I've got this." Akiko took her AK-47 and followed Daphne.

Daphne ran up the stairs and around the corner to the rooms they had stayed in. The barricade had collapsed. A pile of deaders several feet deep sat on this end of it. She tried to climb over, but Akiko yanked her back.

"Are you nuts?"

Daphne glared at her. "What?"

Akiko pointed to several moving deaders amongst the pile.

Daphne circled around the southern side of the motel and approached their rooms from the rear. Akiko stayed with her.

She checked each room, including the bathrooms, continually calling Paul's name. When she did not find him, she then examined the deaders around the barricade. There was no human blood. And no sign of Paul.

Daphne crawled up on the railing.

"What are you doing?"

"He may be on the roof."

Akiko sighed. "At least let me help you."

She steadied Daphne as the latter boosted herself up and peered over the edge.

"Any sign of him?"

"No. But he left his ammo bag. He wouldn't have done that unless he was in trouble."

Daphne climbed up on the roof, retrieved the bag, and futilely searched the area for any signs of Paul.

"Paul!"

The only response was groaning from the deaders trapped in the pile.

She climbed back down to the exterior corridor with Akiko's help. When back down, Daphne peered over the railing and blanched. She bolted for the rear stairwell and ran down, making her way to the pile of dead below. Akiko followed. Ed and Lisa joined her.

"What's wrong?" asked Lisa.

Akiko shrugged.

Daphne reached over the mass of dead and picked up Paul's Vepr. It was covered in gore.

Ed closed his eyes and muttered a silent prayer.

"Paul wouldn't have left this here if he was...." Daphne broke down into tears.

Akiko stepped over and hugged her, hoping the act of affection would lessen the pain.

Without warning, Daphne pushed Akiko away, took the Vepr and bag of ammo, and ran back upstairs to where the deaders still moved in the pile in front of the barricade. A deader in nurses' scrubs made eye contact with her and snarled. Daphne aimed the shotgun at its head, screamed, and fired. Its head exploded.

Lisa tried to follow, but Ed stopped her.

"She needs this."

The three stood in the lot, watching Daphne vent her anger and grief on the living dead. When those still moving were eliminated, she reloaded and fired into the corpses, crying out every few seconds. After the third reload was used up, she yelled "motherfuckers" at the top of her lungs, fell back against the wall, slid into a fetal position, and sobbed.

ONCE DAPHNE HAD cried herself out, Akiko and Lisa went up to comfort her, and then brought her back to the vehicles. She sat in the passenger seat of the Pilot and said nothing. Akiko stayed with the kids, who had no idea how to react. Gojira went over, crawled into Daphne's lap, and cuddled with her.

When it was time to leave, Daphne pleaded to search the hotel one last time to make certain Paul wasn't hiding somewhere wounded or, if he had turned, give her the chance to put him out of his misery. Akiko and Lisa stayed with the kids while Ed followed her through the hotel. It took over an hour before they gave up the search and returned to the rest of the group.

Daphne walked to the center of the lot and stared into the woods, so emotionally drained she could no longer cry.

"I hate the idea of him wandering around as one of the living dead."

Lisa placed her hands on Daphne's shoulders. "Come on, hon. We need to go. I'll drive."

She helped Daphne into the passenger seat and climbed in behind the wheel. Ed drove the RAM.

Pulling out of the parking lot, the convoy turned onto Brownsburg Turnpike and continued west. Daphne turned in her seat and stared at the motel until it was no longer in view, then sat forward and lowered her head, sobbing quietly.

They had driven less than ten minutes when Lisa laughed.

Daphne glared at her. "What's so fucking funny?"

Lisa pointed ahead of them and smiled. "That."

An electronic sign used to warn drivers of road conditions up ahead sat on the shoulder. The orange lights carried a unique message.

DAPHNE

MEET ME AT LEXINGTON VALLEY VINEYARDS

IT'S NOT FAR FROM HERE

PAUL

Preview of
Nurse Alissa vs. the Zombies X: Endgame

Colorado Springs, Colorado

THE FEMALE DEADER shambled down the street, oblivious to where it was or where it was going.

The milky glaze that covered its eyes greatly diminished its vision, creating a blurred world of shadows. It detected movement off to its right, somehow different from the shambling of the hundreds of thousands of living dead roaming the city. The female deader turned and staggered toward it, only to bump into something solid. It did not realize it had walked into one of the few unbroken glass storefronts still left in the city, nor did it comprehend that what it had spotted was its own reflection. All that mattered was this was not food.

The female deader backed away, leaving chunks of decayed flesh from its nose and forehead stuck to the surface, then studied the blurred image. It had no concept that it stared at its own image. It wore what was once an attractive tan skirt and matching jacket, both stained with dried blood and several months of dirt. The white satin blouse and pearl necklace around its neck were in the worst shape, soiled with blood and pieces of decayed human flesh torn from its victims. Its long auburn hair, now matted and filthy, hung in clumps off its head. The deader had long since lost its high heels. Its nylons were in tatters, especially around the right leg below the knee where chunks of flesh had been chewed off during day one of the outbreak, the bite that eventually turned it. When human, the woman would have been extremely attractive.

Now, it was just one of the horde of deaders infesting the city.

The female deader stumbled along on its bad leg, sensing no pain. Everything human about it had long since been stripped away. It lacked emotions. It possessed no memories of its past life or its existence since becoming one of the living dead. It did not experience exhaustion from walking around endlessly for months or feel the discomfort from its bare feet that had been worn down to the bone. Nor did it realize its body was slowly rotting away and would eventually fall apart, its limbs no longer functioning, leaving it to lay wherever it fell until the brain decayed enough to end the thing's existence. The elements that slowly ravaged its body, the rain and snow, the heat and cold, meant nothing to it. Like all the living dead, it sensed only one thing.

An insatiable hunger.

Like every other deader in the city, it had not eaten in several months.

As one, the horde groaned. The female deader cocked its head. A noise in the distance cut through the silence, growing louder as it rapidly drew closer. None of the living dead knew what made the noise or recognized the sound as belonging to a car engine. It did not matter. Their primordial minds had learned that any sound meant one thing.

Food was nearby.

A lone SUV raced through the city. It contained a father, mother, and three children who had ridden out the apocalypse on their farm outside of Castle Rock but had to abandon it when a horde of the living dead displaced them. The father drove at a high speed, avoiding the deaders he could and crushing any that got in his way. Since the horde had dissipated over time, the family was fortunate to make it through the city without being overwhelmed. When they finally reached the city's southern outskirts, the father accelerated, putting as much distance as possible between themselves and the famished horde. They were safe.

For now.

The slow, steady decay prevented the horde from moving fast, allowing the family the opportunity to escape. However, if the lack of physical pain and emotion gave the living dead any advantage, it was persistence. The family had been the only food the dead had seen in months, and the horde was not about to let it go without a struggle. The deaders along the main thoroughfare began to move in the direction the SUV had gone, shuffling along on decaying legs. Those on the side streets and neighborhoods fell into line and followed, a pack mentality having taken over. Within an hour, every deader in the city was on the move.

By nightfall, the mega-horde, numbering close to one million living dead, surged south along I-25.

A Thank You to My Readers

I love writing. It's one of the most fulfilling things I've done. And of all the subgenres I write in, zombies are my favorite.

The best part of writing is having fans who love reading about her adventures and the many dear friends I made on my journey. I'm incredibly fortunate and grateful to have a fanbase that devours my novels like zombies eating human flesh. You keep reading, and I'll keep writing.

I'll make the same request I always do at the end of all my books. If you liked it, or any of the books I have written, please leave a review on Amazon and Goodreads, tell your friends, and promote it on any zombie book lover sites you may be on. The review doesn't have to be lengthy—just a rating and a sentence or two about why you enjoyed it. The more reviews the series receives, the more opportunity other readers have to discover the book.

If you're looking for a zombie fix, don't forget my other series, *Nurse Alissa vs. the Zombies*. There are already nine books in the saga. I've begun drafting the last book in the series, which will be released later this year, so you have time to get caught up on them before the explosive conclusion. Unlike *The Chronicles of Paul*, which has a *Dead Rising* feel, the Nurse Alissa books are more serious.

See you next book.

Acknowledgments

I know I say this at the end of every novel, but that's because it's true. The fun part of my job is writing. The difficult part is publishing the books, with editing at the top of my frustration list. It's a complicated process. Thankfully, writers are not alone through it all, and those who help out deserve to be recognized.

Many thanks also go out to my beta readers, Doc Fried and Dungeon Dan Uebel, who have been with me since book one. They point out grammatical/spelling errors and inconsistencies and offer their opinion on whether they like the story. I would be lost without them. Like all my others, this book is a much better read because of them.

As he does with both my zombie series, Christian Bentulan designed the cover for *The Chronicles of Paul III: Road to Nowhere*. His work perfectly fits the mood of these books. I enjoy collaborating with him.

As always, a major debt of thanks goes to my furry family. Working from home allows me to set my hours, though it's rare if I work less than ten hours a day. But it also means my pets are with me all the time and demand constant attention. Fred, AKA Turd Burglar, my Beagle-Bassett puppy, is always with me when I write, and sometimes I spend more time keeping him out of trouble than I do at my computer. At night, while editing and managing social media, my cats Archer and Michonne stand in front of my desktop computer, Michonne because she wants to be petted, and Archer because he ran out of treats or can see the bottom of his food dish. I love them all.

About the Author

Scott M. Baker was born and raised in Everett, Massachusetts, and spent twenty-three years in northern Virginia working for the Central Intelligence Agency. He has traveled extensively through Europe, Asia, and the Middle East, incorporating many of the locations and cultures in his stories. Scott is now retired and lives outside Salem, New Hampshire, with his dog Fred and two cats who treat him as their human servant.

Scott is currently writing the *Nurse Alissa vs. the Zombies* and *The Chronicles of Paul* sagas, his latest zombie apocalypse series, as well as his Tatyana paranormal series. Previous works include *Operation Majestic*, his first science fiction novel described as *Raiders of the Lost Ark* meets *Back to the Future* – with aliens; *Frozen World*, his first non-zombie post-apocalypse novel; the *Shattered World* series, his five-book young adult post-apocalypse thriller; *The Vampire Hunters* trilogy, about humans fighting the undead in Washington D.C.; *Yeitso*, his homage to the giant monster movies of the 1950s that he loved watching as a kid; as well as several zombie-themed novellas and anthologies.

Amazon Author's Page: amazon.com/stores/Scott-M.-Baker/author/B003N4U9BK
Facebook: facebook.com/groups/397749347486177
Twitter: twitter.com/vampire_hunters
Instagram: instagram.com/scottmbakerwriter
Blog: scottmbakerauthor.blogspot.com/
YouTube:
youtube.com/channel/UC5AyCVrEAncr2E0N5XoyUdg/featured
Wyrd Realities Homepage: www.wyrdrealities.net

You can also sign up for Scott's newsletter, which will be released on the 1st and 15th of every month. He promises not to share your email with anyone or spam the recipients. The newsletter contains advance notices of upcoming releases/events and short stories from the Alissa, Paul, and Tatyana universes that will not be available to the public. You can sign up by going to the link below.

Newsletter: mailchi.mp/0b1401f1ddb2/scott-m-baker-writer